New TOEIC Listening

PART 1

Book 6 上課實況

1. (C) (A) The waiter is <u>taking</u> an order. 變成 ing 的規則

    (B) A diner is <u>making</u> a reservation. ① close → closing

    (C) A chef is <u>pouring</u> oil into a pan. 誰有, 去掉 e, 在 e 有 ing

chief 顧長官 (D) A manager is posting a schedule. ② lie → lying

    die → dying

2. (C) (A) The man is climbing the stairs. 誰有 ie, 去 ie + ying

    (B) The man is climbing a tree. ③ 單音節 + 短母音, 重複字尾 + ing

    (C) The man is climbing down a ladder. sit → sitting

    (D) The man is climbing up a ladder. put → putting

    ④ 雙音節 + 重音 + 短母音 → 重複字尾

    begin → beginning

3. (A) (A) The woman is exercising on the floor. control → controlling

    (B) The woman is cleaning a toilet.

    (C) The woman is watching TV.

    (D) The woman is making a phone call.

    ＊ tie n. 領帶; 聯繫, 束縛

    n. 輪胎 v. 裝輪胎 → She says the house work

4. (C) (A) The man is changing a tire. is a tie. 是個牽累。

    (B) The man is changing a battery. v. 拴, 捆, 約束

    (C) The woman is changing a lightbulb. → I was tied

    (D) The woman is changing her clothes. to my job

    /taɪ/ by a contract.

5. (A) (A) They are in a business meeting.

    (B) They are at a sales seminar.

    (C) They are on an airplane.

    (D) They are near the ocean.

    waterski n. 滑水橇

6. (A) (A) A man is waterskiing. v. 滑水

    (B) Some people are enjoying their food.

    (C) A girl is crying. sew v. 縫合; 縫上

    /so/

    (D) A woman is <u>sewing</u>. → All the details of the project

    安排完成, 確保...成功 have been sewn up.

    /son/

    控制 → I want to have the election sewn up

    even before I put my name on the list.

GO ON TO THE NEXT PAGE.

PART 2

7. (B) <u>Where's</u> the best place around here to get some pizza? 複數N·規則
   (A) I think it could have been better.
   (B) Have you tried the pizzeria on Jackson Street?
   (C) A bag of potatoes.

8. (C) Why are so many people coming in late today?
   (A) No, the deadline is next week.
   (B) I drive to work.
   (C) The transit workers went on strike.

9. (B) Has your phone number changed in the past year?
   (A) No, there's no entry fee.
   (B) Yes, I switched <u>carriers</u> last month.
   (C) I left it at home.

10. (A) Should I make a reservation at the Japanese restaurant or the Korean one?
    (A) <u>Either</u> one <u>is</u> fine with me.
    (B) Call the restaurant for directions.
    (C) I missed my flight.

11. (B) When do we need to be at the airport?
    (A) In Seattle.
    (B) By seven-thirty.
    (C) Several times.

12. (B) Who will distribute the promotional <u>materials</u>?
    (A) No, I didn't.
    (B) Mr. Patterson will.
    (C) The address is <u>www.openbook.com</u>.

13. (C) Did you see the prices on the merchandise?
    (A) I think I have room for one more.
    (B) A table for three, please.
    (C) Yes, everything is quite expensive.

14. (C) You've met Gerald and Pam before, haven't you?
    (A) Let's meet there.
    (B) It starts tomorrow.
    (C) No, I haven't.

15. (C) Where's the nearest post office?
     (A) It was interesting.
     (B) It leaves from platform B.
     (C) There's one across the street.

16. (A) Would you like to join us for lunch?
     (A) That would be great.
     (B) Pasta, I think.
     (C) Yes, it's made of steel.

分辨的出来 made of
分辨不出来 made from
→ Their houses were made of the trees they had cut down.

17. (C) How long was Ms. Whiteside on vacation?
     (A) It's too short.
     (B) At the doctor's office.
     (C) Only for a week.

→ The cider is made from apples.

18. (C) Why are all our desks in the hallway?
     (A) Yes, take the elevator downstairs.
     (B) On my desk is fine.
     (C) The main office is being painted.

*paint
n. 油漆,涂料
v. 涂颜色,画 The boy is painting a cat.
→ paint over sth.
We'll have to paint over the dirty marks on the wall.

19. (B) What's the airfare for a non-stop flight to Miami?
     (A) At the airport.
     (B) About 500 dollars.
     (C) For six hours.

*suggest
暗示 = hint
= imply
= intimate
= insinuate (暗测,迂回的说)
→ She insinuated to us that Tom had cheated on Annie.

20. (C) Are you giving your presentation this morning or in the afternoon?
     (A) Thanks for the suggestion.
     (B) A short presentation.
     (C) It's today at two.

up. 回建议 = advise
= propose

21. (A) Who should we send the contract to?
     (A) All parties involved.
     (B) Print it on both sides.
     (C) By express mail.

*express
v. 表达;挤：The doctor expressed poison from her wound.
n. 快车,快递

22. (B) You are scheduled to work at the front desk on Sunday, aren't you?
     (A) Did she run there?
     (B) No, I'm off the rest of the week.
     (C) They make a good team.

adj. 快递的,明确的
→ The doctor gave express orders.
→ They painted the house for the express purpose of selling it.

GO ON TO THE NEXT PAGE

23. (A) Doesn't Sandra Park live in Phoenix?
    (A) Yes, she's been there a long time.
    (B) No, I've never tried it.
    (C) It's closed for the season.

n. 季, 時候
⇒ It's not the season for quarrels.
現在不是吵架的時候
v. 調味 (with)

24. (C) Can I help you find something in your size?
    (A) There's another seating at six.
    (B) I enjoyed it very much.
    (C) That would be great.

⇒ She seasoned the fish with sugar and vinegar.
使適應
⇒ She was seasoned to outdoor work.
in season 當季
You'll know in season 時間到了你便知道了

25. (C) When are the inventory reports due?
    (A) Because it's a large facility.
    (B) We can't afford it.
    (C) Not until the last day of October.

n. 目錄,庫存品 v. 整點

* until ①. 直到～為止
② 用於否定,直到～才,在～以前
⇒ She didn't go to bed until 11 o'clock.

26. (A) Which office are you going to request?
    (A) I haven't decided yet.
    (B) We'll see about that.
    (C) We're moving next week.

conj. 1'1

27. (C) Do you want to discuss the project now or after the meeting?
    (A) From the project manager.
    (B) Nothing for me, thanks.
    (C) Sorry, I'm busy right now.

a barrel of fun 十分好玩
a barrel of money 好多錢
①. 大桶 ②(D)大量,許多

28. (B) How many barrels of this wine were produced?
    (A) For the summer clearance sale.
    (B) We produced twelve hundred.
    (C) It's a great food pairing.

* pair n. 一對
v. 配對; 組成對
⇒ They paired John and Mary for the game.

29. (A) I can't get the intercom to work properly.
    (A) Here, let me help you.
    (B) Sixty-five copies.
    (C) I don't know how to get there.

n. 對講機

30. (A) Why don't we stop by the pub later?
    (A) Sure, if you want to.
    (B) It stops at the corner.
    (C) Yes, half an hour.

順道前往經過

31. (A) Don't you have the same smart phone as Annette?
    (A) Yes, but mine is the latest model.
    (B) Sometimes I do.
    (C) I always call at that time.

PART 3

Questions 32 through 34 refer to the following conversation.

M : I'm sorry I didn't get back to you yesterday, Jessica. I've been busy planning the reception dinner for Mr. Wright. It's an important event.

W : I know. It's not often we get a visit from one of our top corporate executives. The reception is this Friday night at 7:00, right?

M : Yes, and it's being held at The Russian Tea Room, so... just a reminder. Formal wear is required.

W : Oh, no. I have to be out on a job site that afternoon. So I'll have to go home and change first. I might be a little late——is that OK?

32. (C) What is the main topic of the conversation?
    (A) A conference presentation.
    (B) A building renovation.
    (C) A reception for an executive.
    (D) A budget review.

33. (B) What does the man remind the woman to do?
    (A) Arrive early at an event.
    (B) Dress appropriately.
    (C) Check an account.
    (D) Reserve a table.

34. (A) What will the woman be doing on Friday afternoon?
    (A) Working outside of the office.
    (B) Hosting an event.
    (C) Interviewing a job applicant.
    (D) Meeting a client.

Questions 35 through 37 refer to the following conversation between three speakers.

W : This is Lucy from research and development in the Granger Building. We were supposed to get a package from the Pittsburgh laboratory last week, but it never arrived.

GO ON TO THE NEXT PAGE

USA M : Hang on a second. Hey, Joe! Did we receive a package from Pittsburgh? It's Lucy from R and D. 猜等一下.

Research and Development 研究發展部門

AUS M : No. I haven't seen anything.

USA M : OK, Tony says he hasn't seen anything. If you give me the tracking number, I can check our database. That will tell us if it's in the system and still in transit.

包裹追蹤碼

仍在運送當中

資料庫　*順帶一提*

W : The tracking number is K-T-1-7-9. By the way, I was told by the technician that the package is white and has a shiny blue logo on the side. That would certainly distinguish it from the plain brown boxes we usually receive.

技術人員、技師

USA M : Thanks for that information. As soon as I find out your package's whereabouts, I'll let you know.

adj. 簡樸的, 清楚的, 坦白的, 一般的 ⇒ The child has a plain face.

35. (D) What is the purpose of the call? 　⇒ I must be plain with you.
   (A) To purchase some supplies. 供應品 ⇒ The meaning of the sentence
   (B) To return some merchandise. 生活用品 is very plain.
   (C) To make shipping arrangements.
   (D) To locate a missing item.

36. (A) What does the American man ask for?
   (A) A tracking number.
   (B) An inventory amount.
   (C) The location of a building. ＊otherwise
   (D) The weight of package.

   ①(以)用別的方法
   ⇒ We'll get there somehow,
      by boat or otherwise.

37. (D) What does the woman say about the box?
   (A) It is larger than average.
   (B) It may have been damaged. ②相反的情況
   (C) It is needed soon. He says he was at the cinema,
   (D) It is not brown. but I know otherwise.

Questions 38 through 40 refer to the *following conversation.*

W : I'd like to reserve a table for three on the evening of April 4th, please. Are there any tables available in the first seating? 預訂一張3人桌 table available 可預約的位子

M : Yes, I have one table for three at 5:30 p.m. first seating 第一輪餐座

W : Oh, that's too early. Is there anything a little later? I'm meeting some clients at the airport at 5:00. With traffic, there's no way we can be there by 5:30.

M : Well, I could hold the table for you until 5:45. Would that give you enough time? Otherwise, I have tables available starting at 7:30.

38. (D) What is the woman inquiring about?

    (A) A payment option.

    (B) A ticket upgrade.

    (C) A flight schedule.

    (D) A dinner reservation.

inquire
詢問，調查，求見
+about +into +for
= ask
= question

39. (C) What does the woman say she needs to do at 5:00 p.m.?

    (A) Give a presentation. 做簡報

    (B) Rent a hotel room.

    (C) Meet some clients. 和客限面

    (D) Catch a connecting flight. 搭轉機

38.(A) 付費方法
(B) 票務升級
(C) 飛機行程
(D) 晚餐預約

40. (C) What does the man say he can do?

    (A) Cancel a reservation. 取消一個預訂

    (B) Take a later flight.

    (C) Hold a table. 保留一個桌位

    (D) Contact a client.

Questions 41 through 43 refer to the following conversation.

M : Hi, I see that the community recreation center offers family memberships. Are there any benefits other than pool and tennis court access?

W : Yes, the center has members-only events such as aerobics and art classes every week. Most of our events are appropriate for children and adults of all ages.

M : Count us in. Can I apply for a family membership for six people, please?

W : Sure. Please fill out this form with the names to be included in the membership and your contact information. It will take only a few minutes to print out your membership cards.

41. (B) Where does the conversation take place?

    (A) At a library. 社區，社會，團體 = student /ethnic community

    (B) At a community center. 界 = academic /business /scientific community

    (C) At a concert hall.

    (D) At an aquarium. 水族館

42. (A) What additional membership benefit does the woman mention?

    (A) Special classes.

    (B) Gift certificates. 禮券

    (C) Free parking.

    (D) Discounted merchandise. 打折過的商品

GO ON TO THE NEXT PAGE

43. (C) What does the woman ask the man to do?
   - (A) Present photo identification. n. 識別身分證
   - (B) Return at a later date. 表格 identify v. 確認, 辨識, 認同
   - (C) Complete some paperwork. the same 把...視為同一物
   - (D) Pick up a visitor's guide.

   ⇒ Never identify wealth with happiness.
   He identifies beauty with goodness.

Questions 44 through 46 refer to the following conversation.

adj. 自由放養的

M : Hello, I'd like to buy this whole chicken. Is it free-range?

W : Yes, it is. In fact, these birds are particularly special. They're locally raised just down the 當地養的
   road from here, at Daisyfield Farms. *plump 特別地特別
   v. 拍鬆 : She plumped the cushions.

M : That's great. I'm happy to support local farmers. These birds look so plump and juicy. I'll
   take two, please. adj. 豐滿的, 胖嘟的 : The baby has rosy plump cheeks.

W : Certainly. Would you like some recipes? There are free cards over there that you can take
   if you'd like. 想要一些食譜嗎? 有免費的食譜卡可以拿

44. (B) Where is the conversation most likely taking place? 最有可能在哪裡發生
   - (A) At a restaurant.
   - (B) At a butcher shop. 肉販; 屠夫; 劊子手
   - (C) At a dry cleaners. 乾洗店
   - (D) At a tourist center. → 遊客中心

45. (C) According to the woman, what is special about the product?
   - (A) It is currently discounted. 目前有在打折的
   - (B) It is available today. 只有今天有賣
   - (C) It is locally raised. 是當地養的
   - (D) It is new this season. 是這季新款

46. (D) What does the woman offer the man?
   - (A) A business card. 卡片   *recipe n. ① 食譜
   - (B) An area map. 這區的地圖   ② 方法: He thinks the recipe
   - (C) A handmade basket. 手工的籃子   for success lies in hard work.
   - (D) Free recipes.

drive
n. 轉動; 車程; 努力
宣傳活動 a sales drive

Questions 47 through 49 refer to the following conversation.
n. 善舉; 施捨; 慈善團體; 慈悲; 仁心. out of charity 出於好心

M : Hi, Sophia. Jack Owens here. Listen, since you helped at the company's recycling drive
   for charity last year, I thought you might want to volunteer again this year. It's on Saturday
   and Sunday, the 3rd and 4th of next month. 由於你去年幫助公司的慈善回收活動

W : I'd be glad to help out. I'm free Saturday afternoon.
   很高興能幫上忙   有空

M : That's what I was afraid of. I'm way over-staffed on Saturday afternoon. But we're desperate for people on Sunday morning. Are you available at any time that day?

W : Sorry, I can't do it on Sunday. I wish I could help out, but I think you'll have to find someone else this time.

47. (A) Why is the man calling?
    (A) To recruit staff for an event.
    (B) To find a substitute for a night shift.
    (C) To ask for donations.
    (D) To cancel an advertisement.

48. (A) What does the man mean when he says, "That's what I was afraid of"?
    (A) He expected the woman's response.
    (B) He didn't understand the woman's response.
    (C) He feared the woman's reaction.
    (D) He didn't appreciate the woman's reaction.

49. (C) What will the man have to do?
    (A) Create a job description.
    (B) Reschedule a training session.
    (C) Try to find another volunteer.
    (D) Work the shift himself.

Questions 50 through 52 refer to the following conversation.

M : Hello, Ms. Biggs, this is Luke Ledesma, the building superintendent. We'll be doing routine maintenance in your apartment later this week——just servicing the ventilation systems, checking the smoke detectors, and such. And I'd like to find out when is the best time for us to come.

W : Actually, I'm leaving for vacation tomorrow. And I won't be back till next Sunday evening, so I won't be here when you're doing the maintenance.

M : That's not a problem. I can let the workers into your apartment. The only thing I'll need you to do before you leave is move your furniture away from the vents, so they'll be easier to get to.

50. (D) Why is the man calling?
    (A) To offer a new product.
    (B) To follow up on an estimate.
    (C) To inquire about a lease.
    (D) To arrange a maintenance visit.

GO ON TO THE NEXT PAGE

53

51. (C) What does the woman say she will be doing tomorrow?
  (A) Looking at apartments.
  (B) Attending a workshop. 參加工作坊
  (C) Going on a trip. 去旅行
  (D) Hosting a party. 舉辦派對

52.(A) 繳交訂金
  (B) 完成一項調查
  (C) 移動家俱
  (D) Key留在前台

52. (C) What does the man ask the woman to do?
  (A) Make a deposit. to carry out/conduct a survey
  (B) Complete a survey. the result/findings of a survey
  (C) Move some furniture. to get a survey done 房屋檢測)
  (D) Leave a key at the front desk.

Questions 53 through 55 *refer to the following conversation.*

受歡迎的科技報誌

W : Thanks for coming to see me, Steve. As you know, Baker and Associates is expanding and
版本;說法 如你所知的 正在擴張
we'd like to start offering an online version of our popular technology magazine. My
投提
management team would like you to lead the project. Would you be interested? 有興趣樣嗎?
M : Wow, I'd love to. But I have to wonder, why me? There are plenty of people on the staff
成很想一下;猶何認為
who've worked on the tech magazine much longer than I have.
adj.廣泛的·大量的 大量的網路管理經驗 完全能發現有情勢的新發款
W : Yes, but your extensive website management experience is a game-changer. We think this
would be especially useful for launching an online magazine. We're confident that you'll
produce an outstanding product. 指出線上報誌
傑出狀
                    The disease is a game changer
                    to the development plan.

53. (B) According to the woman, what is the company planning to do?
和媒體工司 (A) Merge with a media company. → to receive widespread media affection coverage
合併   medium量   得到媒體關注,報導
總部搬家 (B) Start an online magazine.
       (C) Relocate its headquarters.
贊助當地 (D) Sponsor a local sports team.   * wonder
運動團體   v.納悶.想知道.覺得奇怪,不明白

54. (B) What does the woman ask the man to do? + about/ that
  (A) Meet with a client.
  (B) Lead a project. 領導一個專案   ⇒ We wonder that the little girl is a
  (C) Train some employees 訓練領工   university student.
  (D) Write an article. 寫文章   n. 奇蹟,驚奇
                    ⇒ There was a look of wonder in his eyes.

55. (C) Why has the management chosen the man?
  (A) He is a professional cyclist. cycle +ist 專業的車手
  (B) He has lived abroad. 騎腳踏車的人 他以前曾在國外住過
  (C) He has experience in Web site management. 對網頁管理有興趣
  (D) He has organized many corporate events. 組織過很多公司活動

Questions 56 through 58 *refer to the following conversation.*

W : Hi, this is Judy Sheen, the tenant of apartment 8B at Stratford Place. I wanted to let your office know that I'm going to be moving out at the end of the month. I've been transferred to my company's headquarters in Los Angeles.

M : Well, I hope that's good news for you, but as stated in a lease agreement, we require one month notice before you move out. So you'll still be responsible for the next month's rent.

W : Would it be possible to waive that portion of the rent? I'll be happy to find someone to sublet the apartment when I leave.

56. (B) Why is the woman moving?
   (A) Her lease has been expired.
   (B) She is being transferred to a different city.
   (C) There has been an increase in the rent.
   (D) The apartment offers no parking.

57. (C) What does the woman ask the man to do?
   (A) Contact the moving company.
   (B) Help her move out.
   (C) Reduce a payment.
   (D) Store some of her belongings.

58. (A) What does the woman offer to do?
   (A) Find a new tenant.
   (B) Call the real estate agent.
   (C) Write out a check.
   (D) Sign the lease.

Questions 59 through 61 *refer to the following conversation.*

W : Hey, Rex. The driver who usually delivers our merchandise to Carver's Department Store called in sick this morning. Do you think you can make his two o'clock delivery for him this afternoon?

M : Sure, no problem, but I've never made any deliveries to McCormick's, so I'll need some directions. How do I get there from our warehouse?

W : I suggest taking Interstate 90 to North Lake Shore Drive. You can't miss it. Once you're there, don't forget to have the shipping supervisor sign the delivery confirmation form.

GO ON TO THE NEXT PAGE

59. (D) What does the woman ask the man to do?
- (A) Work overtime. 加班工作
- (B) Prepare an invoice 準備發票　　invoice: is a request for payment
- (C) Schedule an appointment. 安排場約會　receipt: is a proof of payment
- (D) Make a coworker's delivery. 幫同事送貨　treasury invoice 國庫發票

VAT invoice (value-added Tax)
商業稅發票

60. (D) What does the man say he needs?
- (A) Keys to a vehicle.
- (B) A telephone number. 電話号碼
- (C) A price list. 價格表
- (D) Directions to a location. 去某地的指引

61. (B) What does the woman remind 提醒 the man to do?
- (A) Print a document. 印一份文件
- (B) Get a signature. 得到個簽名
- (C) Keep his receipts. 收據留著
- (D) Check some merchandise. 檢查些商品

Questions 62 through 64 *refer to the following conversation and invoice.*

今天這樣就好了嗎?
W : Will that be all for today? Just a new phone and service upgrade? 可以線上付款嗎?

M : I do have one more question before I buy the phone. Can I pay my bill online? I travel a lot
for work and I'm not at home when the bills come. 怕帳單來的時候我不在家
可以註冊一個付款帳號
W : Absolutely. You can set up a payment account on our website. I also recommend
downloading a mobile phone application so you can view the status of your account anytime. APP

M : OK, great. But I changed my mind about the extended warranty. I don't think I really need
it. Could you remove that from my bill?

W : Of course. 可以從我帳單上移到保嗎　延長保固　可以隨時看你戶頭的狀況

62. (A) Who is the woman?
- (A) A store clerk. 店員
- (B) A real estate agent. 不動產經紀人
- (C) A banker. 銀行員
- (D) A teacher. 老師

63. (B) What does the man ask about?
- (A) Additional features. n 特徵/特色/特點/專欄/面貌/容/特色商品
- (B) Online payments.
- (C) Trade-in policies. 折舊換新
- (D) Coverage area. 覆蓋,保險範圍,新聞報導

56

64. (C) Look at the graphic. Which charge will be removed from the bill? 哪項收費應該從帳單中移除
    (A) $75.00.
    (B) $76.56.
    (C) $100.
    (D) $700.

Description	Unit Price	Total
FZR 9980 Silver 16GB GSM	$700.00	$700.00
Two-year Extended Warranty	$100.00	$100.00
Diamond Unlimited Service Plan (monthly) 鑽石級無限服務方案	$75.00	$75.00
Subtotal		$875.00
運送&處理費 Sales Tax		$76.56
Shipping & Handling		$0.00
Total Due		$951.56

Due upon receipt

Thank you for your business!

Questions 65 through 67 refer to the following conversation and notice.
演唱會系列

W : Ray, there's a new concert series opening at the Royal Oak Theater and some of us from work are planning to go. Are you interested? 橡樹;棕色

M : Sure, I've read about the series. Sounds like there's going to be a lot of great music. How much are tickets? 我有看過關於這系列的消息(報導)

W : It depends. Look, here's the information. We already have more than ten people committed to attending, so we should qualify for that price. 有資格 commit send /let go

M : That's certainly reasonable. Would that be for this weekend? 委託: entrust ⊝做
那絕對是合理的 是這週末舉行嗎 = promise = perform

W : Yes, after work on Friday. = pledge = do

M : Is someone going to order the tickets in advance? 有人會先訂票嗎? 事先

W : Lou in the marketing department is. You could give him a call and let him know to include you. ✗exhibit v.陳列 commit to 表態,承諾,承擔義務
n.展示(會) 表現: She exhibited no fear in the face of danger. commit on 就某事發表看法

65. (D) What type of event are the speakers discussing? → He refused to commit himself
    (A) A theater performance. 劇院表演 on the issue.
    (B) A museum exhibit opening. 博物館展開幕
    (C) A photography workshop.
    (D) A live music concert. 作坊;研討會 → 一場現場音樂演唱會

GO ON TO THE NEXT PAGE

57

66. (C) Look at the graphic. What ticket price will the speakers probably pay?
    (A) $15.
    (B) $18.
    (C) $20.
    (D) $25.

Admission Price per Person	
University student	$18
Group of 10 or more	$20
Member	$15
Nonmember	$25

67. (D) What does the woman suggest the man do?
    (A) Pay with a credit card.
    (B) Rent some equipment.
    (C) Leave work early.
    (D) Call a coworker.

Questions 68 through 70 refer to the following conversation and e-mail.

M : Hey, Joyce, are you able to access the Internet from your workstation?

W : Yeah. I haven't had any issues with it lately, Eric. Actually, my connection has been a little bit faster than usual.

M : Well, I can't even connect to it, so I can't read my email. Did anything from Beau with the latest sales report come yet?

W : Just a few minutes ago. Do you want me to send a reply?

M : That won't be necessary but could you print it out for me? I need a copy of the sales report for the meeting this afternoon.

68. (B) Why is the man unable to access his e-mail?
    (A) His password has expired.
    (B) His Internet connection is not working.
    (C) He forgot to update some software.
    (D) He cancelled his Internet subscription.

58

69. (A) Look at the graphic. Who sent the e-mail the speakers are referring to?
  (A) Beau Tremonte.
  (B) Eric Plonkenberg.
  (C) Vivian Wu.
  (D) Joyce Figg.

refer to 提到

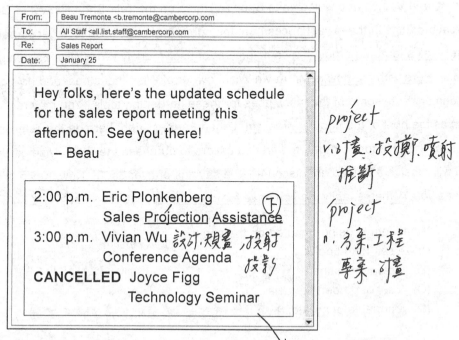

From:	Beau Tremonte <b.tremonte@cambercorp.com
To:	All Staff <all.list.staff@cambercorp.com
Re:	Sales Report
Date:	January 25

Hey folks, here's the updated schedule for the sales report meeting this afternoon. See you there!
– Beau

2:00 p.m. Eric Plonkenberg
                Sales Projection Assistance
3:00 p.m. Vivian Wu
                Conference Agenda
CANCELLED Joyce Figg
                Technology Seminar

project
v. 計畫. 投擲. 噴射
推斷

project
n. 方案. 工程
專案. 計畫

科技研討會

70. (A) What does the man ask the woman to do?
  (A) Print out a document.
  (B) Review some sales figures.
  (C) Inspect his computer. 檢查, 審查
  (D) Prepare some training materials.

(A) 印出一份檔案
(B) 審查一些銷售數字 (圖表)
(C) 檢查他的電腦
(D) 準備一些訓練要用的東西

* assistance
to stand n
站在旁邊輔助
n. 援助
輔助

assistant
人
助手. 助理. 店員
= helper

GO ON TO THE NEXT PAGE

PART 4

Questions 71 through 73 *refer to the following broadcast.*

I'm Athena Vargos and welcome to Shop At Home on the Tele-Shop Network. Get the latest products at the lowest prices from the comfort of home. So let's get started with this week's featured product: a complete set of user-friendly Work Wise gardening tools. Here with me now is Mr. Kevin Wise, owner of Wise Industries, and he's going to demonstrate some of the many uses for these gardening tools. You may recognize him as the host of the popular program "Urban Farmer," right here on the Tele-Shop Network. But before I forget, the first 10 callers to purchase the Work Wise gardening set will receive a 25 percent discount——a savings of over $100! Now, Kevin, it's good to see you. What, exactly, do you have for the viewers today?

71. (C) What item is being featured on the show?
   (A) A self-help book.
   (B) A plant container.
   (C) A set of gardening tools.
   (D) A portable generator.

72. (A) What is Mr. Wise going to do?
   (A) Demonstrate the use of a product.
   (B) Answer questions from viewers.
   (C) Introduce the next guest.
   (D) Show a short video.

73. (D) What is offered to the first 10 callers?
   (A) A ticket to the show.
   (B) Free shipping on an order.
   (C) A club membership.
   (D) A significant discount.

Questions 74 through 76 *refer to the following telephone message.*

Hi, Fiona. It's Richard. Look, I know it's your day-off, but we've got a couple of problems here this morning. We're almost ready to open, but I'm getting worried. Topper's Bakery hasn't delivered our pastries, and Charles hasn't arrived with our dairy order, and we're always his first stop of the morning. I've tried calling but I can't get through to either of them. Don't forget, we have that order of 30 scones and coffee for

Handley Trading at 8:15. Meanwhile, we have enough milk for maybe an hour of the morning rush. After that, we're in big trouble. It's 5:57, and I'm about to open the doors. Please call me back and let me know what to do.

74. (D) Where, most likely, does the speaker work?
- (A) At a convenience store.
- (B) At a talent agency.
- (C) At a brokerage firm.
- (D) At a cafe.

75. (A) What is the problem?
- (A) Some items have not been delivered.
- (B) Some money is missing.
- (C) Some files have been misplaced.
- (D) Some customers are waiting.

76. (C) What does the speaker mean by, "We're in big trouble"?
- (A) They will open an hour later.
- (B) They will fail an inspection.
- (C) They will be out of dairy products.
- (D) They will fire some employees.

Questions 77 through 79 refer to the following talk.

Would everybody please take their seats? OK... I'd like begin this training session for fleet operators of our new Clyster X300 diesel forklifts. You'll notice an attendance sheet is being passed around. Don't forget to include your employee number, so you'll be credited for attending this training. Your 8-digit number is on the back of your company identification card, by the way. After we covered the traffic safety rules of the warehouse floor, I'll walk you through the main forklift routes. When this part of the training session is over, you'll meet our driving instructors who will guide you through your first hands-on experience with the new equipment. Let's get started.

77. (C) What is the speaker about to do?
- (A) Issue identification cards.
- (B) Create work teams.
- (C) Talk about safety guidelines.
- (D) Inspect some equipment.

GO ON TO THE NEXT PAGE

78. (A) What are the listeners asked to provide?
   (A) An employee number.
   (B) A driver's license.
   (C) A personal reference.
   (D) An e-mail address.

79. (B) What will happen at the end of the session?
   (A) A user's manual will be distributed.
   (B) Operators will use the new equipment.
   (C) A supervisor will hand out forms.
   (D) Participants will ask questions.

Questions 80 through 82 refer to the following telephone message.

Hey, Vicki. It's Carl Rogers. We're so lucky you've decided to join us on the logistics committee for this summer's branding conference in Orlando. I just e-mailed you a list of hotels near the conference center. Could you go through the list and contact the hotels underlined about whether or not they can accommodate our team? So far we have 12 associates confirmed for the trip, so we'll need at least 14 rooms. That number could go as high as 20. We'll see. Also, please inquire about meeting facilities at each hotel. We'll want to meet every morning before heading over to the conference. OK. Let me know what you find out and we'll take it from there. I'm at extension 13.

80. (D) What has the listener agreed to do?
   (A) Prepare some training materials.
   (B) Deliver some packages.
   (C) Speak at an event.
   (D) Help plan a conference.

81. (C) What did the speaker send in an e-mail?
   (A) A registration form.
   (B) A tentative itinerary.
   (C) A list of hotels.
   (D) A flight schedule.

82. (D) What is the speaker specifically interested in?
   (A) Price per room.
   (B) Transportation.
   (C) Internet access.
   (D) Meeting facilities.

I'm pleased to officially announce that our merger with Meridian Savings and Trust is now complete. Beginning January 1, our two banks will become Meridian Sterling Bank. We expect this merger to have a substantial and positive impact on you as our employees. First of all, as most of you know, we're relocating to Centennial Tower, located in the heart of downtown, with multiple bus and subway lines. It's going to be much easier on those of you who commute from the suburbs. Additionally, we will integrate many of Meridian's employment policies; for instance, vacation and paid leave. So, all employees will now have three extra days of vacation per calendar year. Sounds pretty good so far, doesn't it?

83. (A) What kind of business does the speaker work in?
   (A) Banking.
   (B) Travel.
   (C) Retail sales.
   (D) Auto insurance.

84. (C) According to the speaker, what advantage does the new location have?
   (A) It has more parking spaces.
   (B) It uses green technology.
   (C) It is easily accessible by public transportation.
   (D) It is close to a variety of restaurants.

85. (C) What policy change does the speaker mention?
   (A) Weekly meetings will be optional.
   (B) Travel expenses will be reimbursed.
   (C) Employees will have more vacation time.
   (D) Telecommuting options will be offered.

This is an automated message to all Kast Construction Company employees. Due to severe weather conditions predicted for Tuesday evening, our Tampa office will be closed tomorrow, Wednesday, July 17. Local weather reports indicate that Hurricane Tina will bring winds of 85 mph after weakening from its Category 2 status Tuesday morning. Despite the weakening, Tina still poses a significant threat to the peninsula.

GO ON TO THE NEXT PAGE.

As a precaution, we're asking all Tampa staff to shut down and completely unplug all electronic devices such as computers and printers. Barring any unforeseen circumstances, the Tampa office will reopen Thursday, July 18. Thank you.

作者 預防,警惕(E) 確保
比如說

86. (A) What is the main purpose of the message?
    (A) To announce a closing.
    (B) To request a deadline extension.
    (C) To report a network issue. 狀況
    (D) To explain a firing decision.

adj. 預料之外的
除了任何意料之外的情況

＊precaution
→ we have taken necessary precautions against fire/flood.
已經採取必要防火/土石流措施。

87. (B) What is expected to happen by the evening?
    (A) New security measures will go into effect.
    (B) Weather conditions will be severe.
    (C) Power will be restored. 法律規則
    (D) Construction will begin.　(生效,實施)

(A) 更新一個行程
(B) 找到一個承包商
(C) 和長官報告要損

88. (D) What are listeners reminded to do?
    (A) Update a schedule.
    (B) Locate a contractor. 立約者,承包商
    (C) Report damage to a supervisor.
    (D) Turn off some equipment.

＊locate
①找出
②把…設在… (D) 把些設備關掉
③使…座落於..

我想用自己的話
來表達歡迎和感謝

Questions 89 through 91 *refer to the following excerpt from a meeting.*

v. 逮捕,追拿 → n. 獵場

Thank you very much, Mr. Franklin. I would like to add my own hello and welcome to everyone and to thank all the members for your wonderful reception when I joined the

超棒的歡迎,當我8月加入董事會時

board in August. To cut to the chase, you've seen our latest budget report. Business

讓我正傳

has steadily decreased in spite of our efforts to attract guests. //Adding insult to injury,

傷口灑塩
↔ Increased

there are plans to build a new hotel across the street.// It's an understatement to say

方法,措施,手段,測量

that drastic measures are in order. Now, I'm sure many of you are hesitant to spend a

adj. 激烈的, 猛烈的, 極端的

lot of money on renovations, but let's face it; our facilities are outdated and our image

is in dire need of a facelift.　→ n. 翻新,整容

adj.可怕的→極度的,緊迫的
為(建築,汽車)
作外觀的改善

underestimate 低估
understatement 不夠/保守的陳述

＊hesitant adj. 猶豫的
here stick hesitate v.
hesitation n.

89. (C) Who are the listeners?
    (A) Engineers.
    (B) Beauticians. 美容師
    (C) Board members.
    (D) News reporters.

90. (D) What does the speaker mean when he says "Adding insult to injury"?
   (A) To emphasize the point.
   (B) To lessen our burden.
   (C) To make a long story short.
   (D) To make things worse.

91. (C) What does the speaker propose?
   (A) Launching an advertising campaign.
   (B) Lodging a formal complaint.
   (C) Renovating a facility.
   (D) Merging with a competitor.

Questions 92 through 94 refer to the following announcement and advertisement.

Attention, Tiger Mart shoppers. This month, Tiger Mart is celebrating its 21st anniversary. In celebration, we'll be having a massive two-for-one blow-out sale in each of our four locations. Here at our store, buy one Wearlite 30-gallon storage box and get the second one free! But please check our advertisement, since each store location has two-for-one deals on different items. And for even more savings, visit our website to become a member of our Tiger Mart Rewards Program. There you'll find all the information you need to sign up and start saving.

92. (C) Look at the graphic. At which store location is the announcement being made?
   (A) Hinsdale.
   (B) Downers Grove.
   (C) Woodridge.
   (D) Burr Ridge.

Tiger Mart Anniversary
Two-for-One Blow Out Sale!

Sales Item	Store Location
Storage Boxes	Woodridge
Water purification filters	Willowbrook
Car wax and polish	Downers Grove
Desk lamps	Burr Ridge

GO ON TO THE NEXT PAGE

93. (C) What is Tiger Mart celebrating?
  (A) A national holiday.
  (B) A profitable quarter.
  (C) An anniversary.
  (D) A new store opening.

*drop off
①〈口〉打瞌睡
⇒ I dropped off and missed the end of the film.
②減少. 掉落
③下車 = Drop me off at the bank.
④走開. 消失: His friends dropped off one by one in the shadows.

94. (D) Why should listeners visit a Web site?
  (A) To check for coupons.
  (B) To write a customer review.
  (C) To vote for the employee of the week.
  (D) To sign up for a rewards program.

Questions 95 through 97 refer to the following telephone message and floor plan.

Hi, Oliver, it's Michelle. I know I asked you to drop off the employee progress reports by the end of today, but I just remembered that I'm going to be at the Baltimore office all day tomorrow. So just go ahead and leave it on my desk whenever you have a chance, and I'll review the reports when I return on Friday. Oh, I just moved to a new office on the sixth floor. To get here, exit the elevator and start heading toward the lobby. Make a right after you pass the reception desk and walk straight. When you reach the bathroom, take another right and I'm the first door on your left.

95. (B) What type of report is the speaker requesting?
  (A) Office inventory.
  (B) Employee evaluations.
  (C) Expense reports.
  (D) Travel receipts.

*lobby n. 大廳，休息室；院外遊說團
v. 對議員進行遊說（疏通）

"Miss Sloane" 電影
Lobbing is about foresight about anticipating your opponent's moves and devising countermeasures.

96. (D) Look at the graphic. Which office belongs to the speaker?
  (A) Office 1.
  (B) Office 2.
  (C) Office 3.
  (D) Office 4.

devise 設計. 想出
Countermeasure 對策, 反抗手段

95.
(A) 新辦公室存貨
(B) 員工評估
(C) 支出報告
(D) 旅行收據

Floor plan: Kitchen, Printing Dept., Elevator, Office 4, Conference Room, Lobby, Bathroom, Reception Desk, Office 3, Office 2, Office 1

97. (D) Why does the speaker postpone a deadline? 為何延期?
   (A) She wants a job to be done thoroughly. /ˈθɜːrəli/ 徹底地
   (B) She needs to interview more people. /ˈθʌrəli/ 認真仔細地
   (C) She knows the listener is busy.
   (D) She will not be able to review some documents until later.
   直到~才~

Questions 98 through 100 refer to the following talk and schedule.

交叉訓練活動

Good morning and welcome back to Day 2 of our cross-training program. Before we begin today's assignment in the personnel department, I'd like to point out a change on 人事部門 / 指出 the schedule. We will be working in the technical support center on Thursday morning. However, Friday morning will now be spent in the warehouse. And remember that this training program includes lunch. Today's meal will be catered by the Italian restaurant 中斷,停止 across the street. We'll break for lunch around 11:45, and then head up to purchasing 十點的 around 1:30.

cater 提供飲食,承辦宴席

98. (B) When is this talk most likely taking place? → He runs a restaurant and also
   (A) On Monday.   caters for weddings and parties.
   (B) On Tuesday.
   (C) On Thursday.   cater to 迎合
   (D) On Friday.

99. (C) Look at the graphic. Which department will listeners visit on Friday afternoon?
   (A) Technical support. 技術支持
   (B) Purchasing. 採購
   (C) Marketing. 行銷
   (D) Personnel. 人事

交叉訓練行程表

CROSS-TRAINING SCHEDULE

Department / Date

Personnel / Monday (a.m.) – Tuesday (a.m.)
Purchasing / Monday (p.m.) – Tuesday (p.m.)
Warehouse / Wednesday
Technical support / Thursday (a.m.) – Friday (a.m.)
Marketing / Thursday (p.m.) – Friday (p.m.)

100. (D) What will happen after the morning session? 早上活動結束後會發生什麼
   (A) Instructors will give a demonstration. 指導員會做展示
   (B) A meeting will be held.
   (C) Identification cards will be distributed. 識別證會被發放
   (D) Lunch will be provided. 午餐會被提供 (有午餐)

GO ON TO THE NEXT PAGE

READING TEST

In the Reading test, you will read a variety of texts and answer several different types of reading comprehension questions. The entire Reading test will last 75 minutes. There are three parts, and directions are given for each part. You are encouraged to answer as many questions as possible within the time allowed.

限定：He has two sisters who work in Starbucks. 他知是有個姊在別處工作

非限定 He has two sisters, who work in Starbucks.

限定用法	補述用法(非限定)
①關代前无逗點	①關代前有 ,
②做受格的關代可省略	②關代不可省略
③可以用 that	③不能用 that

PART 5
他只有2個姊；都在Starbucks工作。

Directions: A word or phrase is missing in each of the sentences below. Four answer choices are given below each sentence. Select the best answer to complete the sentence. Then mark the letter (A), (B), (C), or (D) on your answer sheet.

D 101. Mr. Wang had hoped that the new office would be ------- to the subway station.
(A) closely adv.
(B) closest 最高級
(C) closing 分詞
(D) closer 比較級

C 102. The Viewer Tool offers a wide range of solutions ------- viewing the contents of damaged files of various formats.
(A) as   adj.各式各樣的   版式.設計.格式
(B) in
(C) for
(D) with

非限定(補述用法)前面不是主要句子.後面補述不要也okay

A 103. T.E.K. Consulting is well known for its training program ------- allows employees to switch places with one of their peers.
(A) which   同僚.同事
(B) whose
(C) it
(D) itself

遵守.服從.同意

D 104. To comply with our policy, customers must present a valid sales receipt when returning any -------. adj.
(A) ticket   ①有效的.合法的 a valid contract
(B) survey   the ticket is valid for one week
(C) feature
(D) merchandise ②有根據的.令人信服的
Her argument is valid. 他的論點是站得住腳的

D 105. The mechanic could not repair the car because he did not have the right -------. N.
(A) equip   Please equip yourself with
(B) equipping   a sharp pencil and a rubber
(C) equipped   for the exam.
(D) equipment
v.裝備 準備

D 106. The ------- installed software will decrease the amount of time it takes to pack and ship orders. 不久前才安裝的軟體
(A) fast   會減少打包和寄送訂單
(B) very   的時間。
(C) soon 不久
(D) recently

B 107. Parking fees are charged on weekdays, with both permit and metered spaces available.
(A) while   *split
(B) both   ①切開,劈開
(C) once   ②分攤. He'll split the cost
(D) there   of the dinner between us.

C 108. We will ------- the tasks related to the marketing campaign evenly among all staff members ③均分：We all split equal.
(A) sample   ④揭發：Don't split on me.
(B) suggest
(C) split
(D) suspend

14

109. To reduce glare in the summer months, the building was equipped with the ------- windows available.
(A) darker
(B) darkest
(C) darkly
(D) darkness

110. Most survey participants responded that they ------- watched news programming on Saturday evenings.
(A) alike
(B) instead
(C) rather
(D) seldom

111. ------- of the apartments has its own private entrance.
(A) Such
(B) All
(C) Each
(D) Everyone

112. Business casual attire is considered ------- for the Megatrends Marketing Seminar.
(A) significant
(B) appropriate
(C) useful
(D) complete

113. A new terminal is expected to open at the airport next month, and it ------- for an increase in the number of passengers.
(A) allow
(B) will allow
(C) allowed
(D) has allowed

114. Jefferson Industries is seeking employees with an excellent ------- of both written and spoken Spanish.
(A) excess
(B) description
(C) command
(D) belief

115. The film was received ------- well at the box-office and was one of the biggest hits of the year.
(A) exceptionally
(B) exceptional
(C) except
(D) exception

116. Mr. Brown pays ------- attention to the expense accounts and travel itineraries of the sales team.
(A) particular
(B) substantial
(C) granted
(D) provided

117. ------- pizza boxes are often soaked with grease, they are often not accepted by municipal recycling programs.
(A) Just
(B) Even
(C) Because
(D) In fact

118. Using the latest technology, we're able to offer our customers a wide ------- of printing options to suit their needs.
(A) variety
(B) kind
(C) way
(D) deposit

119. Employees must be aware that their Internet ------- will be closely monitored.
(A) used
(B) uses
(C) usage
(D) using

120. It would be four to six weeks before they would know ------- the marketing campaign was successful.
(A) until
(B) so that
(C) whether
(D) as

121. The goal was ------- more data, from a wider variety of sources, in a shorter amount of time.

S V O. (N詞)

* deteriorate v. 惡化,品質下降

* degenerate

v. 惡退,墮落 adj. 墮落的,墮落的

→ He did not let riches and luxury make him degenerate.

(A) analysis

(B) analyze

(C) analyzed

(D) to analyze 當 S.

122. Each of us took turns thanking Mr. Combs personally on the phone -------- he insisted it was unnecessary.

take turns

(A) as if 猶如,好似

(B) although conj. 雖然,儘管

(C) but

(D) nevertheless adv. 仍然,不過,然而

123. Despite the multiple uses of the product, it failed ------- enthusiasm amongst consumers.

①(介)穿過,儘管,充滿+N ②N.熱誠,熱忱,愛好

The proposal was greeted with great enthusiasm.

受到熱情回應

I = amongst 2 = among

不定詞當補語

(A) generated

(B) generating

(C) will generate

(D) to generate

124. The donation will go toward construction of the business school's new site in the Manhattanville section of New York City.

(π)

(A) toward /vɪ! / - 城,鎮,市

(B) past

(C) near

(D) within adj.專的配套的,整套的

125. The pharmaceutical industry is a highly competitive business and its success is -------
on the marketing and sales of each drug.

/farmə,sjutɪk!/

句已經有v. 所以不會再有 (c) depend

adj.

(A) dependable → Health depends on good food, fresh air and enough sleep.

(B) dependent

(C) depend

(D) depends → It depends on the weather.

126. To prevent milk and other ------- products from deteriorating, ABCO's goods are stored in a cold warehouse.

(A) constructive 建設性的,積極的,有助益的

(B) adverse 相反的,不利的

(C) plentiful 豐富的

(D) perishable 易腐爛的

perish v. 消滅,枯萎

127. Heartland Foods purchased 120 stores from ------- distressed owners.

(A) financing 融資

(B) financial adj. + difficulty 財政困難中

(C) financially 經濟

(D) financed

128. The new monitoring technology empowers people to make continued and ------- improvements to their energy efficiency. n. 效率,功效

授權 准許 使能夠

(A) measurable adj. 可預見的,重大的

(B) vague

(C) severe 嚴重(苛,格,肅)的

(D) prompt 迅速的,敏捷的

129. After ------- with local residents, construction of a new library was suspended indefinitely. 無限期地

hang

(A) deliberate v. 仔細思考 + about/on/upon

(B) deliberation 商議 + with

(C) deliberately

(D) deliberated ① adj. 謹慎的

130. Restaurateurs have been permitted in some jurisdictions to build ------- smoking areas separate from dining areas.

permit 允許

(A) fashioned

(B) featured

(C) differentiated 審判權

n. 司法(權) ((C) 分界線

(D) designated 管轄範圍

區別

mark

designate v. 標出,指定

PART 6

Directions: Read the texts that follow. A word or phrase is missing in some of the sentences. Four answer choices are given below each of the sentences. Select the best answer to complete the text. Then mark the letter (A), (B), (C), or (D) on your answer sheet.

Questions 131-134 refer to the following e-mail.

From: Trask Home Station <info@traskhome.com>
To: Stephan Chicco <c_chicco@intermail.com>
Dear Mr. Chicco,

Thank you for purchasing your new Sontron dishwasher from Trask Home Station. The ------- is scheduled to be delivered to 624 Green
131.

Road on November 5 between 1:00 p.m. and 5:00 p.m. -------. The delivery personnel will unload, uncrate and place the
132.

appliance in the requested room setting.

Your invoice will be sent electronically on the same day.

Please be reminded that we charge $150.00 for orders canceled within

24 hours of delivery or if ------- is at home to accept the delivery.
133.

Please give us a call ------- you have any questions.
134.

---

131. (A) segment
(B) addition
(C) item
(D) detail

132. (A) Delivery will be made by a two-man team trained to install and set up your dishwasher
(B) Appointments will be scheduled three weeks in advance of your session
(C) These hours are similar to those of other restaurants
(D) Customers have already posted some online reviews

133. (A) no one
(B) nothing
(C) neither
(D) not

134. (A) so
(B) that
(C) if
(D) or

GO ON TO THE NEXT PAGE

17

Questions 135-138 refer to the following advertisement.

Global Commerce Insider (GCI) ------- insight
135.
and opinion on international news for 25 years. With its
reputation for thorough analysis of world business and
current affairs, GCI is ------- reading for business leaders as
136.
well as future market leaders.

------- .
137.

To obtain a free trial -------, call (800)-599-5677.
138.

---

135. (A) have been provided
(B) had provided
(C) will provide
(D) has been providing

136. (A) requirements
(B) required
(C) require
(D) requirement

137. (A) A ten-year service agreement includes free oil changes and filters on a monthly basis as directed by your service plan
(B) A two-fold increase of online membership applications is expected to overwhelm our servers
(C) A one-month deposit is required upon signing of the lease, which will be refunded when the lease expires
(D) A one-year subscription comes with online access to world stock market reports updated daily at www.gci.com.

138. (A) standard
(B) right
(C) issue
(D) entry

18

Dear Ms. Larsen,

如同我們上周在電話中討論的
As we discussed on the phone last week, we are going to

評估
meet on May 31 and June 6. We are going to evaluate the

視訊會議系統　　　很重要的是需要知道普遍來說
T-Star videoconferencing system. It is very important to

這個系統是在運作嗎。　　　　effective
find out whether the system has been ------- in general. If

如果需要，　　　to right　我們可以調整系以符合你的需求
necessary, we can adjust the system to suit your needs.
139.

比如說，客戶增加那絡人是有了或是團體會議也可以修改
-------, options for adding contacts and managing group
140.

modify　　　會議還沒發生,用will
sessions can be modified. The meeting ------- at 2:00 p.m.
141.

in your office. -------. I look forward to seeing you on
142.

March 28.

*effect /ɪ'fekt/ n. 效力,效果　*affect /ə'fekt/ (F)
ex make　　　　　v. 實現,產生　v. 影響,假裝

effective /ə'fektɪv/　　　　affection n. 情感; ♡
adj. 有效的,生效的,起作用的　affectation n. 假裝,裝腔作勢

n. 有效性
139. (A) effectiveness
(B) effect n. 結果,作用,影響
(C) effectively
(D) effective

140. (A) Rather　*affect
(B) Even so　v. 影響,假裝
(C) For instance → The amount of rain
(D) Unless　affects the growth of crops.

141. (A) were held → He affected not to see her.
(B) have been held
(C) to hold
(D) will be held

142. (A) Should there be a delay, don't hesitate
to cancel your appointment
(B) If you have any questions or concerns,
please feel free to call me
(C) You can take the shuttle from the
airport to the hotel
(D) Most orders are shipped within 5-7
business days

GO ON TO THE NEXT PAGE.

Questions 143-146 refer to the following article.

涅槃；極樂世界
Nirvana Sound and Vision is the most trusted name in
/nɪrˈvænə/ adj.聽覺的 n.音響裝置
professional audio sales in southwest Oregon. ------- its Since

143.

president Matthew Sands, founded Nirvana Sound and
10年之前.搭配 since   這間公司已建立起很好的顧客服務
Vision 10 years ago, the company has established great
根據 Sands 先生的說法,
customer service. -------. According to Mr. Sands, he -------
recognize v.   144.   他是靠對客戶的特別關注才得到   145.
this recognition by offering personal attention to 現在的名聲
n.諾出;識別;承諾   他相信對待客戶像對待家人一樣
customers. Mr. Sands believes that a focus on treating
會幫助生意發展出一個對於品質和可靠度扎實的
customers like family has helped the business develop 名聲。
reputation
a solid ------- for outstanding quality and reliability.
adj.固體的   146.   * compliment n.恭維,道賀 v.祝賀
廣厚.音調單一的   fill
實心的   complimentary adj.贊貴的,恭維的
圓結的 ⇒ We are solid   * acquaint   v.告知, 使認識
一致的 for peace.   /əˈkwent/
                    acquaintance n.相識.熟人.認識的人

143. (A) When   ⇒ He has many acquaintances   145. (A) was earning
(B) Until   In the business community.   (B) will earn
(C) While   (C) will be earned
(D) Since   (D) has earned

adv.因此,必然地
144. (A) Consequently, Nirvana closed most of its   146. (A) compliment 左
    operations in Oregon   (B) acquaintance 左
(B) Meanwhile, digital audio sales continue to   (C) reputation
    decline adv.期間.同時 n.期間 in the meanwhile   (D) familiarity
比外 (C) Additionally, the company will offer wedding ① 熟悉.通曉 +with
    packages beginning in March   ② 親暱.放肆
(D) In fact, it was rated as the number one
    audio/video retailer in southwest Oregon   ⇒ His excessive familiarity
    this year   made her uncomfortable.

20

Directions: In this part you will read a selection of texts, such as magazine and newspaper articles, e-mails, and instant messages. Each text or set of texts is followed by several questions. Select the best answer for each question and mark the letter (A), (B), (C), or (D) on your answer sheet.

Questions 147-148 refer to the following notice.

ATTENTION CHAPEL HILL HOMEOWNERS

In an effort to reduce our carbon footprint, the Chapel Hill Homeowner's Association (CHHA) is moving online and going paperless. As of September 1, all association-related communications, our monthly newsletter, resident directory, and advisory notifications will be issued via our Web site, at www.chha.org.

Please visit our Web site at your earliest convenience to sign up for our automated e-mail alert system, which will keep you up-to-date with CHHA activities and announcements. Meanwhile, please look over the resident directory to confirm that your information is accurate. Feel free to call me with corrections.

Thanks,

Randall Emerson
Chapel Hill Homeowner's Association
384-0099

147. What change will be made to the monthly newsletter?
(A) It will be edited by a homeowner.
(B) It will cover more than one neighborhood.
(C) It will include advertisements.
(D) It will be available only online.

148. According to the notice, why might readers contact Mr. Emerson?
(A) To subscribe to a newsletter.
(B) To suggest changes in deadlines.
(C) To request a correction.
(D) To list a property for sale.

GO ON TO THE NEXT PAGE.

defect n. 過失；缺失點 v. 逃跑，脫離 → He defected to the enemy. 投敵3
= weakness = flaw → n. 電子學
defection n. 背叛

JC Electronics

electronic adj. 電子的

Our Return Policy

defective adj. 有瑕疵的，不完美的 → He is mentally defective. 心智不健全

- Non-defective products must be returned within thirty days (30)
  down | make
  from the date of purchase, unless otherwise indicated.
  其他的事項   say↑ indicate
  proclaim 指示，表示，顯示

- Returned product must be in original packaging, unused,
  undamaged and in saleable condition.
  退還的貨物要保持原包裝，全新未使用過，未受損，並且還可見良好的狀態

- Proof of purchase is required and all non-warranted items are
  subject to a 15% restocking fee.
  be subject to 受...控制；有...傾向；依照

→ The party is subject to government supervision.
這個政黨受政府監督

→ I have made plans but they are subject to your approval.
需要你的定奪

本篇通知的主旨為何？

149. What is the purpose of the notice?
B
  (A) To announce an event.
  (B) To explain a policy.
  (C) To advertise a product.
  (D) To recruit new employees.
grow

A manufacture v. 製造
hand | make

manumit v. 解放奴隸
send

manuscript n. 原稿，抄本

關於退貨貨品時要求為何？

150. What is stated about items to be
C
  returned?
  (A) A manager must approve the
    transaction. *交易，辦理，處置*
  (B) The price tag must be attached
    to them.
  (C) They are accepted for a limited
    period of time.
  (D) They must be sent back to the
    manufacturer. *製造商/人*

我們在短時間內會聯繫(提)符合您團隊需求的方案和價格

LINK UP Co-working Office: Connect, Network, Inspire

謝你對Linkup公司有興趣

吸氣,鼓舞.激勵.驅使

Thank you for your interest in LINK UP. Please complete the request

form below. We will contact you shortly with the plan and pricing that

will suit the needs of your group. contact v. 與~接觸;與~聯繫

Name: _____ Contact n. 交往,接觸.聯繫 + with

Contact Number: _____ → He tried in vain to get into contact with

E-mail: _____ Phone: the local branch.

Date(s): _____ → He made contacts with wealthy people.

戈門路.拉關係.

Location preference: 西洋杉.雪杉

[ ] LINK UP Cedar Rapids   [ ] LINK UP Des Moines

[ ] LINK UP Davenport adj. 快的.

會員方案   迅速的   * reserve
                                          v. 及物
Membership Plan

[ ] Drop-in/Daily Pass   [ ] Full-time   [ ] Non-profit 儲備,保存,保留

[ ] Corporate (name of organization): _____ 預約.預訂

會員數量   The court will reserve
                                            judgement.
Number of memberships: [ ] Single   [ ] 2-5   [ ] 6+

是否需要商務中心通行權   法庭將延期判決

Business center access required: [ ] Yes   [ ] No

Computer rental: [ ] Yes   [ ] No   n.儲備金(物)

LINK UP Co-working Space: Connect, Network, Inspire 儲備選手.備籌

→ He told us the truth without reserve. 毫無保留地 → He spoke with reserve.

A 151. According to the form, what will
     Crossroads LINK UP staff do?

     (A) Calculate a rate based on the
         information submitted.
     (B) Reserve a conference room.
     (C) Provide discounts for more than six
         memberships.
     (D) Assist participants on the day of an
         event.

D 152. What is true about LINK UP? 他說話語順

     (A) It recently began operating its
         own non-profit organization.
     (B) It requires members to log into a
         Web site.
     (C) It is not accepting new members.
     (D) It has three locations.

GO ON TO THE NEXT PAGE

*vision

Bright Eyes Vision Clinic
98 East 12th Avenue
New York, NY 10012

n.①視力/視覺 ⇒ People wear glasses to improve their vision.
②洞察力/眼光 ⇒ He is a man of great vision.
v. 瞥見, 顯現

April 10

*optometry
sight | measure
n. 驗光 → optometrist n. 驗光師

hyperopia
far | condition
n. 遠視 = farsight

myopia
short
n. 近視 = shortsight

Ethan Feldman
248 Astoria Avenue
Queens, NY 11009

Dear Mr. Feldman:

At Bright Eyes Vision Clinic, the doctors and our entire optometry team are committed to providing advanced vision care in a professional and comfortable environment. 專業且舒適的環境 Therefore, it is essential that your account information be up-to-date. 從5月1號起生效 Effective May 1, all invoices are due within 30 days of service. Please find enclosed a complete and detailed explanation of our revised billing schedule. 所有的發票費用在服務後30天內到期 (30天內要繳清) 修訂;校正

The revision allows us to continue to provide clinical care to you and your family without increasing the cost of services this year. 不會增加今年的金額 Should you need to make alternate payment arrangements, please contact our office manager, George McMahon, at (212)909-1212. 付款安排(付費方法) 替代的

倒裝 = 汗的意思 更正式, 用於強調

154(B) 營業時間更新
(C) 啟用新的經理
(D) 希望避免費用上升

Sincerely,
Bright Eyes Vision Clinic

153(A) 吸引新病人
(B) 宣佈新政策改變

B **153.** Why was the letter sent to Mr. Feldman?
(A) To attract new patients.
(B) To announce a policy change. 經營營運
(C) To reschedule an appointment.
(D) To promote a newly upgraded clinic. 宣傳一間新升級的診所

D **154.** What is indicated about Bright Eyes Vision Clinic? 迎合低收入病患
(A) It caters to low-income patients.
(B) It has updated its hours of operation.
(C) It has hired a new office manager.
(D) It hopes to avoid an increase in fees.

Carlos Betancourt, Recollections, 2010, C-print mounted on Plexiglas, ©
Carlos Betancourt

The first piece from Carlos Betancourt's "Baroque to Bling" series has gained international recognition following exhibitions in museums and galleries around the world, including the Art Institute of Chicago, the Warhol Gallery in Pittsburgh, and the Louvre in Paris. _Recollections_ was featured on the cover of The Atlantic Monthly in September of last year. Originally purchased by Donna McMillan for her private collection, the piece was donated to the Palm Springs Art Museum for our permanent collection last month. The Baroque to Bling works offer contemporary interpretations of the baroque, a term that brings to mind lavishly ornamental design, elaborate aesthetics, and a sense of the theatrical.

155. Where is the information posted?
(A) At the Louvre.
(B) At the Warhol Gallery.
(C) At the Art Institute of Chicago.
(D) At the Palm Springs Art Museum.

156. Who, most likely, is Ms. McMillan?
(A) A sculptor.
(B) An art historian.
(C) An art collector.
(D) A gallery manager.

157. What is NOT stated about Recollections?
(A) It belongs to a series of works.
(B) It has had more than one owner.
(C) It appeared on the cover of The Atlantic Monthly.
(D) The artist considers it to be one of his best works.

GO ON TO THE NEXT PAGE.

Steam Pressure Washer – Grime Fighter- $500 (Cupertino)

Posting Description:

I haven't used this washer in a while; the gun and hoses are missing. Will also need a fuel pump ($50). The unit worked great last year when we used it on the tractor, but the fuel pump has since corroded.

This machine would be well over a thousand if it were in top condition, but since it needs that fuel pump, gun, and hoses, I'm asking $500 or best offer. Welcome to come check it out anytime. As you can see in the pics, it's been kept clean.

Reply to: call or text me for address: 673-5566

158. What is NOT indicated about the pressure washer?

(A) It has had more than one owner.

(B) It has been kept clean.

(C) It needs a new fuel pump.

(D) Its hasn't been used in a while.

159. What is the seller willing to do?

(A) Ship the item to a buyer.

(B) Negotiate a price.

(C) Include an extra fuel pump.

(D) Extend the warranty.

160. What is implied about the ad?

(A) It includes photographs.

(B) It was posted in a newspaper.

(C) It was posted several weeks earlier.

(D) It only applies to residents of Cupertino.

*scout n. 童子軍
→ a good scout 好人
v. 偵察

v. 蝕,遮: The news eclipses everything else.

TREVOR YOUNT: Executive V.P., Global Human Resources

→ to scout the trail 探路

n. 蝕: There will be a Total eclipse of the sun next Tuesday.

找人才

As Eclipse's Chief Human Resource Officer, Trevor's responsibilities include talent
/ˈkɪˈɪps/ 人員發展 激勵 n.保留 基礎建設·公共建設

scouting, development, inspiration, retention and infrastructure planning for all
/aɪ/ 硬體規劃

incorporated

worldwide employees in the Eclipse brand and affiliate organizations (Runverse

Limited Liability Company son v.隸屬於 n. 分區

Inc. and Turley International LLC). Prior to Eclipse, Trevor led the Talent and

在 Eclipse 之前 Trevor 領導 T&P 部門

補償 福利 政策訂定 計畫設計 n. 管理. 經營. 監督

Performance Division at SaberCo. In this role, he was responsible for
compensation and benefits policy setting, plan design and administration for

160,000 employees worldwide and for the company's talent management

他擔任多種國際職位

functions. During his career at SaberCo he held a variety of international

曾待8年國際市場

positions that included eight years based in international markets. Prior to

人力資源部門

joining SaberCo, Trevor led the human resources division for Filmore and Pierce

經濟 和 會計 學位

Management Consultants. Trevor holds degrees from two Ivy League universities

—an economics and accounting degree from Dartmouth College and an MBA

in finance from Harvard. He has more than 20 years of human resource

corporate and consulting experience.

常春藤名校

nominate v. 提名, 任命, 指派
name

Harvard Columbia Pennsylvania
Yale Cornell Dartmouth College
Brown Princeton

161. What is the purpose of the
information? n.主管 adj.行政的; 執行的
(A) To detail an executive's
nomination for an award. 掌管的
(B) To announce the winner of a
competition.
(C) To profile a company employee.
(D) To summarize an employee's
current research.

C

162. What is NOT indicated as one of Mr.
Yount's current responsibilities?
(A) Talent scouting.
(B) Product marketing.
(C) Infrastructure planning.
(D) Employee retention.

B

163. What is suggested about Mr. Yount?
(A) He attended college in Canada.
(B) He was an accountant at SaberCo.
(C) His responsibilities are very broad.
(D) His career is almost over.

C

GO ON TO THE NEXT PAGE.

From:	Mike <m_cleary@currentmail.com>
To:	Kendra <k_fulton@currentmail.com>
Re:	Schedule Update
Date:	May 23

Kendra:

我建議我們再移動一次到下周二,也就是5月31號

Just one quick change to your schedule tomorrow. Your client Lou Pristo

明天下午晚一點

called this evening and requested to reschedule your meeting for later in

明天起身出發

the afternoon tomorrow. Since you're leaving for the conference at 3:30,

你能確認這次的約會嗎?   again   項目

I suggested we move it back to next Thursday, which is May 31. Do you

時間空格   工廠原型

want to confirm this appointment? Also, you'll see that I've filled Mr.

Pristo's time slot with the pending review of the factory prototypes. Let

adj.浮兆的   (n)直到~為止

me know if that doesn't work for you.

懸而未決的 Pending his return, let us get
                                    everything
                                    ready.

Time	Appointment	Attendees
7:45 a.m.	Breakfast @ Over Easy Café 讓我們在他回	Richard Loeb
	來之前把一切	Mai Truong
9:00 a.m.	Team meeting: Midwest Sales Conference 準備好	Lee Vanderburg
		Dina Saedi
11:00 a.m.	Review of factory prototypes	Cole Zendik
Noon	Lunch @ Kingsbury	John Platt
		Dina Saedi
1:45 p.m.	Marketing meeting	Julie Jones
3:30 p.m.	Car service to Lambert-St. Louis Int'l Airport	

飯店和飛機確記所刷好的備份資料放在你的桌上

Meanwhile, printed copies of your hotel and flight confirmation are on your

desk, so you'll see them first thing when you come in tomorrow.

你明天一進辦公室就會看到了

Cheers,

Mike

164. Why was the e-mail sent?

B

(A) To discuss an agenda for a meeting.
(B) To provide a <u>revised</u> daily schedule.
(C) To change a travel itinerary.
(D) To confirm a restaurant reservation.

165. What will most likely happen on May

C

31?

(A) Ms. Saedi will give a presentation at a conference. 會在場會議中做演示
(B) Mr. Spence will purchase a train ticket. 購買一張火車票
(C) Mr. Pristo will meet with Ms. Fulton.
(D) Ms. Moore will return from St. Louis.

166. Which of the following is something

B

Mike Spence has done for Kendra Fulton? 取消一場約會(會面)

(A) Cancelled an appointment.
(B) Printed some documents.
(C) Opened her mail.
(D) Paid for a meal.

167. At what time was Mr. Pristo

C

expected?

(A) 7:45 a.m.
(B) 9:00 a.m.
(C) 11:00 a.m.
(D) 3:30 p.m.

* revise 修正, 校訂

v.及
複習 + for → revise for the exam

LLC : Limited Liability Company —Member
有限責任公司

LTD : Limited Partnership —Partner ① GP: General Partner
② LP: Limited Partner

INC = 股分有限公司
Incorporated

— Tax payer 法人
— Dividend 股息

164 (A) 討論一個會議的議程
(B) 提供一個修訂過的日程表
(C) 改變一個旅行行程
(D) 確認一個餐廳預約

GO ON TO THE NEXT PAGE.

Orion Bicycles

Progress Report for the week of November 8-12

Carla Roberts, Project Lead

This week's progress:

Researched several manufacturing companies in Guadalajara, Mexico, with experience making custom bicycle seats. ---[1]--- Sent schematics of our new seat design and inquired about logistics: minimum order quantity, shipping, production, and turnaround time, ETC. ---[2]---

Based on initial discussions, Avendia Industrias seems to be the manufacturer that will work for us. ---[3]--- Likewise, Juan Garza, the factory sales manager got back to me right away with a detailed quote! He seemed very accommodating and eager for our business. My intuition tells me we'd have a solid business relationship with Avendia.

Contacted four other companies that were either out of our price range or unable to accommodate our schedule. ---[4]--- Thus, no longer in contention for our business.

Plans for the week of November 15-19

Continue discussions with Avendia Industrias about project needs and invoicing terms.

Have the design team outline the steps of the production process.

Submit this information to Avendia so that a prototype can be manufactured.

168. What is suggested about Orion Bicycles? 搬到墨西哥

C

(A) It is relocating to Mexico.

(B) It is hiring a sales manager. 雇用銷售經理

(C) It is developing a new product.

(D) It is closing a facility. 關閉一個地方

改備地方廁所

169. According to the report, what did Ms. Roberts do during the week of November 8?

D

(A) She finalized shipping schedules.

(B) She acquired new machinery. 機器

(C) She interviewed potential factory 政府的機構 employees.

構

(D) She evaluated possible business partners.

170. What is mentioned about Mr. Garza?

D

(A) He will travel to meet Ms. Roberts in person.

(B) He is part of the design team.

(C) He asked few questions.

(D) He is very accommodating.

171. In which of the positions marked [1], [2], [3], and [4] does the following sentences best belong?

C

"They are a relatively new and smaller company, but are willing to hire additional staff to complete our order."

(A) [1]. 這和介紹公司相關的

(B) [2].

(C) [3].

(D) [4].

＊acquire v. 獲得；習得
seek

acquirement n. 獲得；成就；學識

acquisition n. 獲得物 = This dress is Anna's new acquisition.
［ə͵əkwɪ͵ɪʃən］
取得 = He devoted his time to the acquisition of knowledge.

＊What is your sign?
I am a/the _____.

1. 摩羯 (the Goat) Capricorn

2. 水瓶 (the Water Carrier) Aquarius

3. 双魚 (the Fishes) Pisces

4. 牡羊 (the Ram) Aries

5. 金牛 (the Bull) Taurus

6. 双子 (The Twins) Gemini

7. 巨蟹 (the Crab) Cancer

8. 獅子 (the Lion) Leo

9. 處女 (the Virgin) Virgo

10. 天秤 (the Scales) Libra

11. 天蠍 (the Scorpion) Scorpio

12. 射手 (the Archer) Sagittarious

GO ON TO THE NEXT PAGE

Questions 172-175 refer to the following online chat discussion.

Regine Nilo [3:02 p.m.] Tony, something is wrong with the shopping cart on our Web site. It doesn't open when you click on the icon; a customer just called to complain that she can't process her transaction.

Anthony Swift [3:03 p.m.] Uh-oh. When did the problem start?

Regine Nilo [3:04 p.m.] **No clue.** I was alerted by the customer. It's the first I'm hearing about it. Can you get in touch with someone from IT and find out what's going on?

Anthony Swift [3:05 p.m.] Doug, the shopping cart function is down on the Web site. Do you have any idea what's happening?

Doug Rapier [3:06 p.m.] Yeah, one of my programmers entered a line of bad code during routine maintenance. We're looking for it right now.

Anthony Swift [3:09 p.m.] I hope you can get it back up and running soon.

Doug Rapier [3:16 p.m.] Depends, but probably not longer than an hour. I've got the whole team on it.

Anthony Swift [3:21 p.m.] The sooner the better, Doug. By the way, let Regine know when you fix it. I'll need her to write some kind of apology and notification for the landing page.

Regine Nilo [3:22 p.m.] I'm already on it, Tony. Doug, I just emailed you a draft. Can you put it in a small, tasteful banner?

Doug Rapier [3:26 p.m.] Got it. Consider it done. Sorry about the issue, guys. We just found the error, and it should be resolved in the next minute or two when the system is refreshed.

172. What problem does Ms. Nilo report?

C

(A) The company's Web site cannot be accessed.

(B) Some product information is incorrect.

(C) Payments cannot be processed in the online store.

(D) The company's Web site is re-directing customers to another site.

173. From whom did Ms. Nilo learn about

C

the problem?

(A) A consultant.

(B) A supervisor.

(C) A customer.

(D) An IT coworker.

174. What does Mr. Rapier say caused the problem?

A

(A) Human error.

(B) Too much Internet traffic.

(C) A new program.

(D) A technical issue with their service

I

provider. 工藝的，技術的，專門的

175. At 3:04, what does Ms. Nilo most likely

D

mean when she writes, "No clue." T

(A) She is concerned about the sales report.

(B) She has already spoken to somebody in IT.

(C) She has never used the shopping cart function.

(D) She doesn't know when the problem began.

174 (D)

Technical advances improve productivity.

技術進步提高生產力

The job calls for technical skill.

這個工作需要專門技術

175

(A) 她很擔心這份銷售報告

(B) 他已經跟在IT部門的人說過了

(C) 她從來沒有用過購物車的功能

(D) 她不知道問題何時開始的

175

no clue = I have no clue = I don't have any idea.

totally clueless → completely unaware about sth.

and maybe even a little bit silly or stupid

+ about sth.

→ I am totally clueless about social media.

GO ON TO THE NEXT PAGE

From:	g.sterling@panorama.com
To:	d.bernardo@shuttershow.net
Re:	Panorama's Photography Digest
Date:	August 11

Dear Mr. Bernardo,

Panorama's Photography Digest is offering discounted advertising rates to first-time advertisers. For a limited time, when you place an ad in Panorama's Photography Digest, you can reach a targeted audience of over 60,000 photography professionals in print and online. Expand your customer base by taking advantage of this unique opportunity.

Outlined below are our current offers for first-time advertisers, valid until September 15. To reserve any of these full-color advertisements, have one of our designers create a custom layout for you, or request more information, please reply to this e-mail or call me at 404-800-0103 ext. 33. Specifications for advertisements are available at www.panorama.com/ads.

Sincerely,
Gwen Sterling
Marketing Coordinator
Panorama's Photography Digest

From:	d.bernardo@shuttershow.net
To:	g.sterling@panorama.com
Re:	Panorama's Photography Digest
Date:	August 12

他是個品格優秀的人

Hello Ms. Sterling,

"標準純銀 adj. 純正的, 優秀的, 純銀的 →He is a man of sterling character.

I received your e-mail and am interested in placing an advertisement in Panorama's Photography Digest. However, I need some clarification about the online advertisement. The specifications on your Web site are unclear about the location of the advertisement. Where exactly would the 4"x5" advertisement appear on your Web site? 網站上關於地點的詳細描述不清楚

請你一有空便回覆我

Please get back to me at your earliest convenience, and I can provide an electronic file of the advertisement together with my credit card information.

Thanks,

A clarify
v. 澄清, 闡明: He clarified his stand on this issue.
淨化: It requires great efforts to clarify sewage in cities.
使清楚, 清澈

Doug Bernardo
Owner

=His muddled brain suddenly clarified. 污穢物
/sjuːɪdʒ/ 污水

176. Why did Ms. Sterling e-mail Mr. Bernardo?
(A) To inform him of a special promotion.
(B) To offer him a discount on a subscription.
(C) To announce the launch of a publication.
(D) To advertise a new agricultural product.
field adj. 農業的

177. What is suggested about Panorama's Photography Digest?
(A) It publishes a full-color magazine. 出版
(B) It recently expanded its readership. 擴展閱讀群
(C) It will be releasing a special issue. 推出一個特別的刊物
(D) It has increased its advertising rates.

178. What is implied about Mr. Bernardo?
(A) He has never advertised with Panorama.
(B) He will be out of the office in October.
(C) He is a graphic designer.
(D) He has worked with Ms. Sterling before.

179. In the second e-mail, the word "unclear" in paragraph 1, line 3, is closest in meaning to
(A) on hold.
(B) in doubt.
(C) at once.
(D) for certain.

180. What concern does Mr. Bernardo have?
下一本刊物的期限
(A) Deadline for the next issue.
(B) Placement of the advertisement. 廣告的布置(位置)
(C) Appropriate digital file type.
(D) Size of the page. 適合的數位檔案數型

糊塗腦子
突然清醒 A

GO ON TO THE NEXT PAGE.

From:	t.chou@thompsondigital.com
To:	r.harvey@bullseye.net
Re:	Thompson Digital Marketing – Graphic Design
Date:	Wednesday, June 9

Dear Ms. Harvey,

We enjoyed meeting you during our interview on Monday and believe you will be a tremendous asset to the graphic design team at Thompson Digital Marketing. You will provide creative support in the creation and analysis of marketing and communication deliverables, including, but not limited to brochures, direct mail pieces, onsite collateral, signs and banners, website graphics, print ads, social media, e-mail campaigns, and other visuals. You will execute and maintain high quality sales collateral based on direction and branding of the company.

Your assignment will commence in July with a two-day training session at our headquarters in Palo Alto, California. We're hoping to select a time that's convenient for as many people on the new team as possible, especially those like you who will be moving from out-of-state. Please respond to this e-mail as soon as possible and let me know what starting date in July you prefer.

This is a contract position, and aside from the initial training session, work will be done remotely, meaning you are free to set your own hours and schedule. As discussed, design projects are compensated at a variable rate depending on the complexity of the assignment. Marsalis Tull, our head of human resources, will be in touch soon with all the necessary documents you will need to fill out.

We look forward to working with you!

Tiffany Chou
Thompson Digital Marketing

From:	t.chou@thompsondigital.com
To:	All Graphic Designers *demand exceeds availability 供不應求*
Re:	Thompson Digital Marketing – Graphic Design
Date:	June 9 *available adj. 有用的, 可得到的; 可買到的*

→ Is there water available around here?
有空的 → The director is available now.
買得到的 → The ticket is no longer available.

Dear Graphic Design Team,

根據你的回饋(應)

Based on your feedback, it appears that July 16-17 works best for most of you. Please note that training will run from Saturday morning through Sunday afternoon. We expect anyone who lives outside the area to arrive on Thursday, July 14, when we will arrange for you to have dinner with some of our local designers if you like. All travel 所有的旅行 expenses will be covered by Thompson Digital Marketing. More 開支/公司會 details about this will follow, but for now I just want to inform you of 買單 the schedule so you can put it on your calendars. 可以放在行程表上

Tiffany Chou
Thompson Digital Marketing

issue
n. 問題, 爭議. 子女 → He died without issue.
(土地, 地產) 收益
v. 發行, 發佈, 配給, 流出 → Lava issued from the volcano.

181. Why did Ms. Chou write to Ms. Harvey?
(A) To promote a writing workshop. 作坊, 小研討會
(B) To negotiate a salary. 討論薪水
(C) To offer her a position. 小工廠
(D) To provide technical assistance. 提供技術支援

182. What information is Ms. Harvey asked to provide? 目前客戶的名單
(A) A list of her current clients.
(B) Her educational background. 她的教育背景
(C) Her availability for training. (V) 訓練時是否有空
(D) A summary of her work experience.

183. Why will Mr. Tull contact Ms. Harvey?
(A) To issue employment paperwork (V) 發給員工一些紙本資料
(B) To explain software requirements.
(C) To clarify a company policy.
(D) To make travel arrangements.

184. What is indicated about graphic design projects?
(A) They are assigned on a weekly basis. assign 分派, 指派
(B) Some are needed on a daily basis.
(C) Some are more difficult than others.
(D) They are paid a flat fee upon completion. 固定的薪水, 價格

185. What will Ms. Harvey most likely do on July 14? 文件夾, 投資組合
(A) Submit a graphic design portfolio.
(B) Travel to Palo Alto.
(C) Participate in a training session.
(D) Meet Mr. Tull.

GO ON TO THE NEXT PAGE.

From:	Olivia Harrison <o.harrison@redstar.com>
To:	Service <bills@pacificgas.com>
Re:	Invoice #OHAR834-PP234
Date:	June 10

To whom it may concern:

I am writing about my gas bill for May. You've billed me for $310.87, which is substantially higher than what I have been invoiced in previous months. For the record, I have never been late or missed a payment, nor was I notified of a price increase, so I would like to know the reason for the sudden increase in the amount. If the amount has been billed in error, I would appreciate an adjustment to my account.

My gas meter is old and I've long wondered if it should be replaced. If a technician needs to check it, the best time would be before noon on any weekday. I prefer to be present if possible while the work is being done.

Kind regards,
Olivia Harrison

Pacific Gas
Service Technician Log Sheet—Clayton Ridge Residences
June 15

Technician name	Address of service	Start time	Service
Samir Shah	249 Walker Cir.	9:22 A.M.	Meter repaired
Joe Petsche	1082 Plainfield Rd.	10:38 A.M.	Meter replaced
Sloane Sherwin	1145 Cherry Tree Ln.	1:31 P.M.	Meter replaced
Brandon Glover	87 Laurel Canyon Rd.	3:17 P.M.	Meter inspected

From:	Service <bills@pacificgas.com>
To:	Olivia Harrison <o.harrison@redstar.com>
Re:	Invoice #OHAR834-PP234
Date:	June 16

Dear Ms. Harrison,

Thank you for contacting Pacific Gas. We have determined that a faulty meter had registered your usage incorrectly. The technician who visited your Plainfield Road residence this morning replaced the meter, and the problem should not occur again. The malfunction affects your bill for April only.

A credit in the amount of $150.70 will appear on your next bill.

If you have any question, please do not hesitate to contact us.

Sincerely,
Francine Force
Medit Power Customer Support

186. Why was the first e-mail sent?
(A) To sign up for online billing.
(B) To inquire about a charge.
(C) To ask for a deadline extension.
(D) To request a receipt.

187. What is suggested about Ms. Harrison?
(A) She has never missed a payment.
(B) She has recently moved to a different house.
(C) She has contacted Ms. Force repeatedly.
(D) She has multiple accounts with Pacific Gas.

188. Who visited Ms. Harrison's house on June 15?
(A) Mr. Shah.
(B) Mr. Petsche.
(C) Ms. Sherwin.
(D) Mr. Glover.

189. In the second e-mail, in paragraph 1, line 2 the word "usage" is closest in meaning to
(A) habit.
(B) condition.
(C) fee.
(D) amount.

190. What does Ms. Force indicate in her e-mail?
(A) A payment is now overdue.
(B) A new service is being offered.
(C) A new meter has been ordered.
(D) A problem was limited to one month.

GO ON TO THE NEXT PAGE.

Rocky Mountain Council for Industry & Commerce
6th Annual Solid Waste and Recycling Symposium
Parkway Plaza Casper Convention Centre
Casper, Wyoming
Saturday, April 12

Tentative Schedule

Time	Location	
	Location	
9:15 A.M. - 9:45 A.M.	Welcome and Opening Remarks by RMCIC President Buck Stratham Moresche Banquet Hall	
	Wind River Room	Grand Teton Room
10:15 A.M. - 11:45 A.M.	Beneficial Use of Drill Cuttings in Land Reclamation – Wallace Vicker	Creating Standards of Excellence for Safety and Quality – Devin Paul Trevino
1:30 P.M. - 2:30 P.M.	A Generator's Perspective to Hazardous Materials Disposal – Sunny Stiles	Implementing Mobile Laser Scanning in Solid Waste Engineering – Tanner Cody
3:15 P.M. - 4:45 P.M.	Ash Facility Management: What's In & What's Out? – Maryanne Campbell	Can Landfill Gas Cause Groundwater Contamination? – Thanasis Pashalides

• Presenters must notify Walter Dorgan (w.dorgan@rmcic.org.) of needed changes by March 30. A final version of the schedule will be posted by April 5 on our Web site, www.rmcic.org/schedule

• Presenters MUST register for the event. Select the "Registration" tab on our Web site and fill out a registration form. Be sure to mark the box labeled, "Presenter." Additionally, those planning to recruit personnel should complete an Employer Application, available under the site's Career Center tab.

• The Parkway Plaza Days Inn has a limited number of rooms still available at a discounted rate, so consider booking promptly.

From:	Maryanne Campbell <m.campbell@campbellash.com>
To:	Walter Dorgan<w.dorgan@rmcic.org>
Re:	Schedule change request
Date:	March 30

*circumstance n. 情況
②事情：His arrival is a happy circumstance,
③細節：with great circumstances

Dear Mr. Dorgan,

由於無法控制的情況產生

我的 同事

Due to circumstances beyond his control, my colleague, Thanasis

不能夠做他的演出了

Pashalides, is unable to give his presentation. I have now been

接管，繼任

asked to take over from him. Looking at the most recent draft of

空格
(行程表上的)

the conference schedule, however, I noticed that the time slot

strike
格子

assigned to Mr. Pashalides conflicts with mine. Kindly, assist me

conflict ✓
conflict n. 鬥爭，衝突，

in resolving this dilemma. Thank you.

困境，進退兩難

Sincerely,

Maryanne Campbell

* sophisticate
wise
v. 使世故，複雜化
n. 世故的人
* sophistication
n. 世故，複雜，教養
* sophisticated
adj. 世故的，有經驗的，精通的

{ freshman
sophomore   moros
foolish
junior
senior

* capacity
n. 容量，容積，
能量，生產力 an annual capacity
of 1200 cars
能力 + for
地位，職位 + as

GO ON TO THE NEXT PAGE

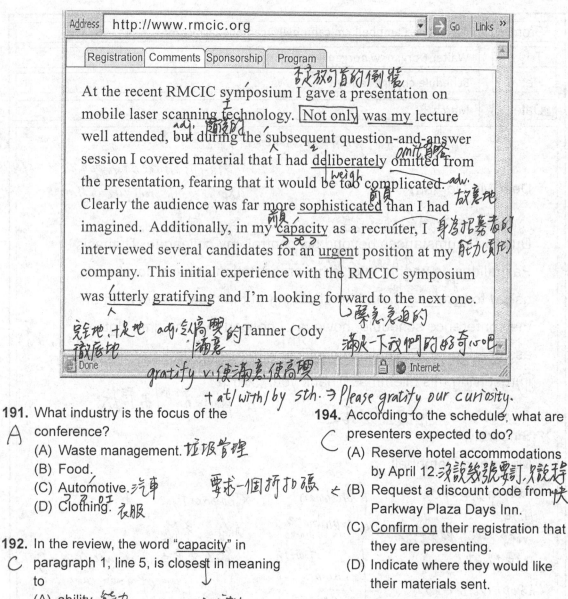

At the recent RMCIC symposium I gave a presentation on mobile laser scanning technology. Not only was my lecture well attended, but during the subsequent question-and-answer session I covered material that I had deliberately omitted from the presentation, fearing that it would be too complicated. Clearly the audience was far more sophisticated than I had imagined. Additionally, in my capacity as a recruiter, I interviewed several candidates for an urgent position at my company. This initial experience with the RMCIC symposium was utterly gratifying and I'm looking forward to the next one.

Tanner Cody

191. What industry is the focus of the conference?

(A) Waste management.
(B) Food.
(C) Automotive.
(D) Clothing.

192. In the review, the word "capacity" in paragraph 1, line 5, is closest in meaning to

(A) ability.
(B) solution.
(C) role.
(D) time.

193. What has Ms. Campbell been asked to do?

(A) Arrange a meeting with Mr. Dorgan.
(B) Submit a draft of her presentation.
(C) Substitute for another presenter.
(D) Cancel travel arrangements made for Mr. Cody.

194. According to the schedule, what are presenters expected to do?

(A) Reserve hotel accommodations by April 12.
(B) Request a discount code from Parkway Plaza Days Inn.
(C) Confirm on their registration that they are presenting.
(D) Indicate where they would like their materials sent.

195. What is probably true about Mr. Cody?

(A) He preferred the recent RMCIC conference over previous ones.
(B) He believed his topic would be easy to understand.
(C) He recently opened an ash management company.
(D) He filled out an Employer Application when registering.

=hot thermal adj.熱的 thermos n.熱水瓶

THERMO KING COLDCASE CONTAINERS contain v.包含(含),控制 =I can't contain my laughter.
Mobile Refrigerated Storage Units
移動式的   adj.經濟的,節約的   → 受歡迎 =desired =coveted
We provide mobile refrigeration rental units of various sizes and capacities depending
on the needs of the client. Our prices are economical, and this makes our mobile 裝置
refrigeration rental company much sought after by restaurants, food distributors,
grocery stores, and other businesses looking for cold-storage solutions. All units include
lockable door latches, non-slip flooring, and interior fluorescent light fixtures, and all
門閂   地板   /fluəreʃnt/
are equipped with a 60-foot power cable. Our units can be delivered to any location in
Texas and are available for short-term hire, monthly rental, or **annual** lease.

Unit	Door Type	Length (feet)	Floor space (square feet)	Internal capacity (cubic feet)
Economy	Single	5	25ft^2	125ft^3
Standard	Double	8	64ft^2	512ft^3
Deluxe	Double	15	225ft^2	3375ft^3
Deluxe Plus	Double	20	400ft^2	8000ft^3

豪華的高級的
/dɪˈlʌks/

Whether your needs are temporary or long-term, our knowledgeable customer service
representatives can recommend the ideal storage solution for you. For more
information, visit http://www.thermoking.com

THERMO KING COLDCASE CONTAINERS — Customer Inquiry Form

n.詢問,調查,打聽
/ɪz/

→ They held an inquiry into the incident.

Name: Sasha Lee
Business: Sasha's
E-mail: sasha@sashastampa.com   → He answered all my inquiries.
Date: July 22
inquire v.調查 into
詢問 about
求見 for

Comments: 大到能走進的   使適合容納
I heard about your company from a friend, Avi Gregorius, who rents one of your
units for his business, Avi's Delicatessen. I am also a restaurant owner, and our
walk-in freezer can no longer accommodate us. Thus, we require an additional
Thermo King Coldcase unit that can be placed near the loading dock behind our
building. We don't need a lot of extra storage space, but we do need a unit with
two doors so we can easily load everything in and out. Please let me know which
unit you recommend and when you can deliver it. Also, please tell me if your units
contain a digital temperature display. We need to be able to closely monitor the
temperature at all times. Thank you. I am at your service at all times.隨時為您效勞

每時每刻.永遠

GO ON TO THE NEXT PAGE

Customer Review

I am very satisfied with my Thermo King Coldcase storage container, and I was quite pleased to have my first month's rental fee waived thanks to Thermo King's refer-a-friend program. I started with a smaller, 512 cubic-foot **storage** unit, but it became clear this month that I would need something one size larger. So I called Thermo King, and within a couple of hours, my sales rep, Joe Irwin, showed up with a new, larger unit. I highly recommend Thermo King Containers to all business owners for whom cold storage is a necessity.

- Sasha Lee, owner, Sasha's

196. What information about Thermo King storage units is NOT included in the advertisement?
(A) The range of temperature settings.
(B) The amount of interior space.
(C) The number of doors.
(D) The type of lighting.

197. What is probably true about Mr. Gregorius?
(A) He used to work with Ms. Lee.
(B) He owns a franchise.
(C) He plans to hire another butcher.
(D) He received a discount from Thermo King Containers.

198. What is suggested about Sasha's?
(A) Its business continues to grow.
(B) It is located near Avi's Delicatessen.
(C) It plans to extend its operating hours.
(D) Its menu features locally grown foods.

199. Which storage container is Ms. Lee currently using?
(A) Economy.
(B) Standard.
(C) Deluxe.
(D) Deluxe Plus.

200. In the review the phrase "showed up" in paragraph 1, line 5, is closest in meaning to
(A) lifted.
(B) arrived.
(C) increased.
(D) uncovered.

Stop! This is the end of the test. If you finish before time is called, you may go back to Parts 5, 6, and 7 and check your work.

New TOEIC Speaking Test

Question 1: Read a Text Aloud

 **Question 1**

Directions: In this part of the test, you will read aloud the text on the screen. You will have 45 seconds to prepare. Then you will have 45 seconds to read the text aloud.

Those who think education has little bearing on success throw out the names of famous university dropouts like Bill Gates and Steve Jobs while proponents of a college degree quote statistic after statistic to prove its impact on a person's employability and earnings. People with experience but no formal degree could be favored for certain jobs, but they may struggle to advance professionally. On the other hand, a college grad with the best education and book smarts may be completely at sea when it comes to dealing with real-world work situations with no prior industry experience, and struggle to land that first job.

PREPARATION TIME
00 : 00 : 45

RESPONSE TIME
00 : 00 : 45

GO ON TO THE NEXT PAGE

Question 2: Read a Text Aloud

((● 5 ●)) **Question 2**

Directions: In this part of the test, you will read aloud the text on the screen. You will have 45 seconds to prepare. Then you will have 45 seconds to read the text aloud.

Japan is building the world's fastest supercomputer, which it hopes will make the country the new global hub for artificial intelligence research. The supercomputer is expected to run at a speed of 130 petaflops, meaning it is able to perform a mind-boggling 130 quadrillion calculations per second (that's 130 million billion). Once complete, the AI Bridging Cloud Infrastructure (ABCI) will be the most powerful supercomputer in the world, surpassing the current champion, China's Sunway TaihuLight, currently operating at 93 petaflops.

Question 3: Describe a Picture

 Question 3

Directions: In this part of the test, you will describe the picture on your screen in as much detail as you can. You will have 30 seconds to prepare your response. Then you will have 45 seconds to speak about the picture.

PREPARATION TIME
00 : 00 : 30

RESPONSE TIME
00 : 00 : 45

GO ON TO THE NEXT PAGE

Question 3: Describe a Picture

答題範例

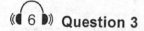

Some people are posing for a picture.

They appear to be having a party.   appear to ✓ / that   似乎；好像

They appear to be in a nightclub.

所有的人除3某人，都有戴眼鏡
All but one person in the picture is wearing sunglasses.

Four people are holding champagne glasses.   ✱occasion
n. 場合，時刻
They are all well-dressed.   重大活動，盛典

n. 閃光, 小發光物 → n. 五彩紙
There is glitter and confetti in the air.

The woman on the left is wearing a party hat.

The guy in the middle has his arms out and palms facing upward.

中間的男人把手伸向外並且手掌向上 ↗

They are most likely celebrating a special occasion. ⚫

很有可能在慶祝一個特殊的活動
If I had to guess, I'd say it's New Year's Eve.

They look abnormally happy, but it is a party after all.

不正常的，反常的 → 看起來太高興3
The people are all smiling or have happy expressions.

Before the picture was taken, they were probably dancing.

It is impossible to say for sure but it looks like their champagne

glasses are empty.

迷人的，富有魅力的
The people are glamorous and attractive.

The women appear to be looking toward the ceiling.

The man second from the right is the tallest of the group.

Questions 4-6: Respond to Questions

 **Question 4**

Directions: In this part of the test, you will answer three questions. For each question, begin responding immediately after you hear a beep. No preparation time is provided. You will have 15 seconds to respond to Questions 4 and 5 and 30 seconds to respond to Question 6.

Imagine that you are participating in a research study about your sleeping habits. You have agreed to answer some questions in a telephone interview.

Question 4   你每晚都有睡足建議的7-8小時嗎？
Do you get the recommended 7 to 8 hours of sleep per night?

> RESPONSE TIME
> 00 : 00 : 15

Question 5   你認為對於你的生活方式來說，你的睡眠時間是足夠的嗎？
Do you feel that the amount of sleep you get is enough for your lifestyle?

> RESPONSE TIME
> 00 : 00 : 15

Question 6   你會如何評價你的睡眠品質，你睡得安穩嗎？
How would you rate the quality of your sleep? Do you sleep soundly at night?

> RESPONSE TIME
> 00 : 00 : 30

GO ON TO THE NEXT PAGE.

Questions 4-6: Respond to Questions

答題範例

🎧 6 **Question 4**

Do you get the recommended 7 to 8 hours of sleep per night?

Answer

{ beyond / above } exception 無可非議

Yes, I generally do.

例外的人/事

There are <u>exceptions</u> of course.

If I don't get enough sleep, I <u>make up</u> for it on the

weekend.

① 補足

② 虛構：The whole story is made up.

③ 組成：The medical team was
made up of 12 doctors.

🎧 6 **Question 5**

Do you feel that the amount of sleep you get is enough for your lifestyle?

＊ I spend a lot one month and not so much the next
and in the end it balanced out.

Answer

Don't worry, things will balanced out.

Yes, I think I get the right amount of sleep.

I'm busy, but not too busy to get enough rest.

I have an active lifestyle but it all <u>balances out</u>. 平衡了

Questions 4-6: Respond to Questions

《 6 》 **Question 6**

How would you rate the quality of your sleep? Do you sleep <u>soundly</u> at night?

ˌsoʊ

Answer

① 健康(全)的：She is sound in body and mind. ⑤ 酣暢地：
② 完好的 = safe and sound　　　　　　　She is a very sound
③ 明智的 = I act on her sound idea.　　　sleeper.
④ 紮實的：He has a sound knowledge of science.

On a scale of 1 to 10, I'd rate the quality of my sleep to

be about an 8.

有時候(偶爾)　我會有點睡不著
Occasionally, I will have a hard time falling asleep.

It's usually because I'm excited about something that will

happen the next day. 對於明天要發生的事情很興奮

一旦我睡著後
Once I fall asleep, I'm out like a light. 我一旦睡著了，就像火燈沒有光
我有設2組不同的鬧鈴，以確保我會 一樣
I have to set two different alarms to make sure I wake up
(睡死了)
on time in the morning.　　　　　　　 = suitable

　　　　　　　　　　　　　　　　　　　= adequate
It's sometimes difficult to wake me.
② adj. 尚可的　　　　　　　　　　　　= sufficient

→ His work is satisfactory but not ① adj. 令人滿意的
　　　　　　　　　　　good.
Overall, the quality of my sleep is very satisfactory.
　　　　　　　　　　　　　　　 ˌsæ tɪs ˈfæk tə rɪ

If I'm feeling particularly tired, I'll make sure to take a nap

or go to bed early. 如果我覺得特別疲累，我會確保自己
小睡一下或是早點上床休息
I'm much more productive when I'm well-rested.

GO ON TO THE NEXT PAGE.

Questions 7-9: Respond to Questions Using Information Provided

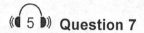 **Question 7**

Directions: In this part of the test, you will answer three questions based on the information provided. You will have 30 seconds to read the information before the questions begin. For each question, begin responding immediately after you hear a beep. No additional preparation time is provided. You will have 15 seconds to respond to Questions 7 and 8 and 30 seconds to respond to Question 9.

Riverside Food Co-Op
coop /kup/ 籠子、棚舍 農場分享引意
Announcing our new Farm Share Program
訂冊農場分享活動可以得到這些的處

Riverside Food Co-Op in Riverside, California, invites you to participate in its community-supported Farm Share program. Members enjoy fresh farm produce during our growing season from April to November.   n.農産品   produce v. 生產、製作 /prə'djus/

Register for Farm Share and receive these benefits:

- Lifetime membership in the Riverside Food Co-Op, giving you direct access to local growers and vendors   variety n. 變化 當季的   柑橘類   /ɜbs/ n. 草本植物
- More than 25 varieties of in-season vegetables, fruits, and herbs, harvested by local producers and delivered fresh to your home by our staff   harvest 收穫(割)"收成
- A selection of pick-your-own citrus fruits, bananas and avocados, and other fruits 成果
- Access to our member Web site with Food Co-Op updates and a Farm Share newsletter
- Discounts on events at the Co-Op for the annual summer music festival. Events cost $15, but members pay $10.   *The new medicine is the harvest of thirty years' research.*

Members receive a farm share once a week. A full-size share is $675, and a half-size share is $350. Half-size shareholders receive half of the full-sized share of produce each week. Our farm produce is locally-grown without the use of pesticides and herbicides. All producers are Certified Organic. For more information or to sign up for a share, please visit our Web site, www.riversidefood.org
有認證的、公認的

    Hi! This is Randy Morris. I'm calling about the food co-op. Would you mind if I asked a few questions?

PREPARATION TIME
00 : 00 : 30

Question 7	Question 8	Question 9
RESPONSE TIME	**RESPONSE TIME**	**RESPONSE TIME**
00 : 00 : 15	00 : 00 : 15	00 : 00 : 30

Questions 7-9: Respond to Questions Using Information Provided

答題範例

((6)) Question 7

農場分享計畫何時會發生

When does the Farm Share program take place?

Answer

從四月到11月

The Farm Share program is active from April to November.

This is related to the growing season. 和生長季有關

We do not operate during the winter months.

冬天不運作

((6)) Question 8

農場分享的東送多久一次，多少錢?

How often do Farm Share shipments arrive and how much are they?

Answer

整個計畫周程中一週一次

Once a week for the duration of the program.

A full-size share is $675, and a half-size share is $350.

股東(不是真正股票.是指可以分農產品的人

Half-size shareholders receive half of the full-sized share

of produce each week.

GO ON TO THE NEXT PAGE

《 6 》 **Question 9**

What are some of the benefits of the Farm Share program?

Answer

One benefit is membership in the Riverside Food Co-Op,

giving you direct access to local growers and vendors.

You can choose between more than 25 varieties of

in-season vegetables, fruits, and herbs, harvested by

local producers and delivered fresh to your home by

our staff.

We also have a selection of pick-your-own citrus fruits,

bananas and avocados, and other fruits.

You'll get access to our member Web site with Food

Co-Op updates.

You'll receive a Farm Share newsletter.

You'll also be eligible for discounts on events at the

Co-Op for the annual summer music festival.

→ Only citizens are eligible to vote.

Question 10: Propose a Solution

《❮ 5 ❯》 **Question 10**

Directions: In this part of the test, you will be presented with a problem and asked to propose a solution. You will have 30 seconds to prepare. Then you will have 60 seconds to speak. In your response, be sure to show that you recognize the problem, and propose a way of dealing with the problem.

＊回答當中要包含兩項

In your response, be sure to ①表現出你瞭解打電話者的問題

- show that you recognize the caller's problem, and
- propose a way of dealing with the problem.

②並且提出處理(解決)問題的方法

PREPARATION TIME
00 : 00 : 30

RESPONSE TIME
00 : 01 : 00

GO ON TO THE NEXT PAGE

Question 10: Propose a Solution

答題範例

🎧 6 🎧 **Question 10**

Voice Message

Hello. This is Mick Sweeney. Two days ago, I ordered

2 從你們網站訂了3兩本書,是用隔日到貨的服務

three books on your website with the next-day delivery,

保證

which guaranteed my books would be delivered to my house
×3
隔天會到。 為了特殊車送(快車到貨)服務我多付了

by the following day. I paid extra for the special delivery
錢

because I wanted those books before I leave the country in

如同你們網站所敘述的   如果訂單是在下午1點前下的

two days. As stated on your website, if the order is placed

應該當天已經收到或是最晚昨天

before 1 p.m., you should have received the order on the

same day and have shipped the books by yesterday at the

latest. Today is already Friday, and I haven't received my
⟵ at the earliest

books yet. Please let me know what happened. You can

contact me on my cell phone at (313) 566-7890.

Question 10: Propose a Solution

☆ confusion
① 困惑: in a state of confusion 答題範例 *③ 混亂: to throw sb./sth.*
②澄清: to avoid confusion *into confusion*

④ 極困惑: To her great confusion,
he asked her to marry
him.

Hello Mr. Sweeney.

This is Jerry Thomas calling you from Booksworld.com.

I am calling regarding your voice message.

You placed an order for three books from our website two days ago with

next-day delivery.

應該

This means you were supposed to receive your books the next day on

Thursday. *很不幸地，你還沒收到你的書*

Unfortunately, you haven't received your package yet.

First of all, I am very sorry for the delivery problem.

I looked up your order record and details, and I don't know why you did

not receive your order the next day. *= uncertainty = Indecision*
= unsureness *(up)*

There must have been some confusion in the delivery system.

It is not very common at all for us to have complaints about our deliveries.

→ 一定是運送系統出了些混亂(狀況)

Anyway, I placed the same order with next-day delivery so you can

have the books by tomorrow.

That way, you'll have them before you leave the country.

And you will also get a refund of the $10 delivery charge as

Booksworld.com credit. *退10吮，可當網站的購物金*

Once again, I apologize for the inconvenience.

If you have any further questions, you can reach me at (313) 340-0500.

Meanwhile, I'd like to ask a favor.

Would you please give me a call once you've received the books?

I'd like to confirm the delivery.

Thank you.

知道問題

解決方法

GO ON TO THE NEXT PAGE

Question 11: Express an Opinion

Directions: In this part of the test, you will give your opinion about a specific topic. Be sure to say as much as you can in the time allowed. You will have 15 seconds to prepare. Then you will have 60 seconds to speak.

If you could study a subject that you have never had the opportunity to study, what would you choose? Explain your choice, using specific reasons and details. 如果你有機會念一個從來沒有機會念的科目 你會選擇哪一個? 解釋你的選擇,用特定的理由和細節。 (詳細的)

PREPARATION TIME
00 : 00 : 15

RESPONSE TIME
00 : 01 : 00

Question 11: Express an Opinion

annotation: ✱ functional
annotation: 答題範例 adj. 功能上的, 起作用的, 實用的
annotation: → The building will be functional from December. 啟用

◖6◗ **Question 11**

annotation: n. 建築學, 結構 → He's barely functional before 10 o'clock.
annotation: 10 點以前需法工作。

I've always wanted to study architecture.

Ever since I was child, I've enjoyed drawing buildings.

At one point, I even drafted a few floor plans.

annotation: adj. 酷的, 現代的, 最新的, 新潮的

Architecture is a creative and artful way to make an impact on society.

After all, architects build modern structures to fit the needs of the world.

They help shape a city through the creation of functional buildings.

Each architectural piece is a creative representation of the thoughts and hopes of the

designer.

Of course, it's important to meet the needs and expectations of your clients.

But the overall look, design and feel of your work is generally a result of your own creativity.

annotation: 很遠的距離

Tourists travel great distances in search of famous pieces of architecture.

The Great Pyramid of Giza, Big Ben, the Golden Gate Bridge, and the Taj Mahal are just a

few world-renowned structures.
annotation: 吉薩金字塔, 大笨鐘, 金門大橋, 泰姬瑪哈陵

Even if I didn't ultimately create the next Eiffel Tower or Empire State Building, my works

would generally be outside, meaning that they would be seen by the public.
annotation: 艾菲爾鐵塔   帝國大廈

Architecture demands attention to detail and focused work.

It is not a data-entry job. *annotation: 數據輸入*

It takes long hours and expertise to create a masterpiece and earn the commission that

comes along with it. *annotation: 專門知識, 技術, 專長   to have / lack the expertise to do sth.*
annotation: 具有/缺乏 做某事的專業知識

If I studied architecture, I would concentrate on larger structures.

I would like to design a museum, or maybe even a hotel.

I think I'd make a good architect. *annotation: his expertise as a builder*

GO ON TO THE NEXT PAGE.

New TOEIC Writing Test

Questions 1-5: Write a Sentence Based on a Picture

Question 1

Directions: Write ONE sentence based on the picture using the TWO words or phrases under it. You may change the forms of the words and you may use them in any order.

＊cart n. 手推車   **push / street**

    ✓運送(用推車) The farmer carted his fruits to the market.

1 The woman is pushing a cart across the street.

2 The woman is pushing the cart from one side of the street
                         to the other.

3. The woman pushing the cart is in the middle of the street.

    ＊ Relationship is a two-way street.

GO ON TO THE NEXT PAGE

Questions 1-5: Write a Sentence Based on a Picture

Question 2

Directions: Write ONE sentence based on the picture using the TWO words or phrases under it. You may change the forms of the words and you may use them in any order.

group / under

a group of 一群的
1 A group of fish ___are___ swimming in the water.
2. A group of kids are under one umbrella.
            crossing the street are under an umbrella.

Questions 1-5: Write a Sentence Based on a Picture

Question 3

Directions: Write ONE sentence based on the picture using the TWO words
or phrases under it. You may change the forms of the words and
you may use them in any order.

judge / gavel 小木槌
æ
（拍賣商，法官，議長用的）

The judge is holding a gavel.

about to strike the gavel.

pointing and holding a gavel.

＊ be about to 即將　　　　　　＊ defeat n. 失敗，挫敗，戰勝
→ We are about to start.　　　① v. 戰勝：The French defeated
→ I am not about to admit defeat.　　the English troops. 軍隊
　　　　　　　　　　　　　　　　　　　　　ㄧㄨㄧ　部隊
　　　　　　　　　　　　　② v. 擊空：Our hopes were
　　　　　　　　　　　　　　　　　defeated.

GO ON TO THE NEXT PAGE

Questions 1-5: Write a Sentence Based on a Picture

Question 4

Directions: Write ONE sentence based on the picture using the TWO words or phrases under it. You may change the forms of the words and you may use them in any order.

✻water n./v. 澆水   **water / garden**

The woman is watering plants in her garden.

The plants in the garden are being watered.

Water is necessary to maintain a garden.

✻ garden path sentence 公園弄句 (弄：苦弄/巷弄)

　　　　　　　　　　双關句子. 一看有錯, 但細看是對的

如: <u>The old man the boat.</u> = The boat is manned by the old people.

　the + adj = 名詞

　man v. 配道

Questions 1-5: Write a Sentence Based on a Picture

Question 5

Directions: Write ONE sentence based on the picture using the TWO words or phrases under it. You may change the forms of the words and you may use them in any order.

collision / head on $<$ adj.

adv. We must meet the problem head-on.

Three vehicles have been in a head-on collision.

Two cars and a truck have collided head-on.

A head-on collision is blocking traffic on the highway.

★ collide v. ①.碰撞 → They collided with another ship.
    ⊗ 91
       ②衝突、抵觸 → If the aim of two countries collide, there may be war.

GO ON TO THE NEXT PAGE.

Questions 6-7: Respond to a written request

Question 6

Directions: Read the e-mail below.

From: Rick Moss <r_moss@tmail.com>

To: Kyle Patrick <deltarunners@yahoo.com>

Subject: Running Club

Sent: Sunday, October 12

Hello Kyle,

fairly
公平地、正當地、處為、相當 *She is a fairly good dancer.*

I found your group online while searching for running clubs in
有任何機會你們還在招收會員嗎?(有可能還在招收嗎?)
Atlanta. Any chance you're still taking members? I'm a fairly
相當地、頗

experienced distance runner, and I'm planning to train for the
即將到來的

upcoming Atlanta Marathon. If you are accepting members, could

you give me some information about the club?
接受會員
(招新會員)

I look forward to hearing from you.
有 +V-ing

Thanks in advance,

Rick Moss

以跑步團體帶領者的身份回信給Rick,邀請他參加並且給他至少兩項
關於這個團體的細節。比如說:何時何地見面等等。

Directions: Write Rick as the leader of the running group. Invite him to
join the group and give at least (2) two details about the
group, i.e. when and where it meets, etc.

Questions 6-7: Respond to a written request

答題範例

Question 6

Rick,

Thanks for inquiring about the Delta Running Club. As it happens, we just had a spot open up and I'd like to invite you to join us. We meet every morning except Sundays in front of the public library on Winslow Avenue in Atlanta. Our group runs normally cover 10k, and we usually separate into sub-groups depending upon levels of endurance, speed, age, etc. Our routes are always posted a week in advance on the Web site, and we encourage club members to suggest new routes. So don't be shy!

As for the size of the group, we've put a cap on 50 people; 50 being the most manageable and productive size, but the actual number of runners who show up every day will vary. However, we are seeking dedicated runners who are either, like yourself, training for an event, or willing to commit to a certain number of days per week.

Let me know if you decide to accept this invitation.

Yours,
Kyle Patrick
President, Delta Running Club

(handwritten annotations:)
詢問
碰巧,偶然
我們有個新點開放
我們在天早上碰面除了周日
君耐力,耐持力
He came to the end of his endurance.
我們的跑步路線通常會一周前公佈
鼓勵社團成員建議新路線
上限50人
至於團體的大小(人數)
忍無可忍了
變多.多樣化
改爭致力的跑者(認真投入)
要嘛
處了活動而訓練
或是願意每週車幾天固定跑步
＊cap = capacity
= (名)最高限度
= 帽子
Whenever he speaks with a lady, he would stand erect, cap in hand
恭敬的站著

GO ON TO THE NEXT PAGE

Questions 6-7: Respond to a written request

Question 7

Directions: Read the e-mail below.

From: Lowell George

Sent: Saturday, May 17

To: Leslie Brown

Subject: Laundry room issues

Leslie,

As your tenant relations manager, I am tasked with reminding you about our standard rules of etiquette practiced in our laundry facilities. I have recently received a number of complaints from residents who have reported their clothes being removed from the dryer and left to sit damp and wrinkled on the counter. The offender is then using the dryer for their own clothing. This is not only rude, but technically criminal, since the dryers aren't free. It's stealing, basically.

While I do not wish to improperly accuse you of any wrongdoing, several residents have pointed the finger at you. Whether or not this is true, I can't say for sure. However, I am compelled to remind you that under no circumstances are residents permitted to touch the personal belongings of others. This is true even if someone has left their clothing in a dryer and the time has expired.

Furthermore, I am now forced to install a security camera in the laundry room in hopes of ceasing this activity. Again, I'm not accusing you of anything. I'm simply reminding you of the rules. If you have any questions, please contact me ASAP.

Yours,

Lowell

Directions: You're upset about the accusation and haven't used the laundry room in six months. Explain why.

Questions 6-7: Respond to a written request

答題範例

Question 7

Hi Lowell,

First of all, I'm offended by the accusations. That certain residents

would point the finger at me for such boorish behavior is not surprising,

given my relationship with some of them. I have a good idea who it is,

though. As you well know, not everybody in the building gets along.

Anyway, the fact is I haven't used the laundry room in over six months;

since I took a new job across town, I'm sending all my laundry to a

cleaning service. In fact, you can check the delivery logs at the front

desk. Honeybee Cleaners. They pick-up on Tuesday and deliver on

Wednesday. So, I definitely couldn't be the person responsible, and

frankly, would never stoop to such petty behavior.

Sincerely,

Leslie

handwritten annotations:

指控

指着我

adj. 粗魯的, 笨拙的

有鑒於我跟他們某些人的關係

相處

We get along just fine.

We can get along without your help.

我把我的洗衣東西(衣物)送去

清洗服務處理

郵寄/飛行日誌

(運送簽收單)

①屈身①弯腰 / +to ⇒ 自貶, 隨落 → I think he'd never stoop to stealing.

* petty adj. 小的, 瑣碎的, 不重要的

→ Don't bother me with such petty things.

②小规模的

→ He was arrested for petty theft.

③下级的

GO ON TO THE NEXT PAGE

Question 8

Directions: Read the question below. You have 30 minutes to plan, write, and revise your essay. Typically, an effective response will contain a minimum of 300 words.

問歷史一個關於過去的問題

If you could ask a historical figure from the past one question, what

明確的 理由

would you ask? Why? Use specific reasons and details to support your

answer.

補充:

① neither 和 nor 常連用

→ I like neither hot dogs nor mustard.

若有三樣東西不喜歡. 同于亦用 nor 連接

→ I like neither hot dogs nor mustard nor ketchup.

② 如果句中有單/複數, 以靠近 nor 的為主

→ Neither the men nor the woman is a good singer.

→ Neither the woman nor the men are good singers.

③ nor 放開頭. 要倒裝

→ I don't usually wake up at 7 a.m., nor do I like to
   wake up at 6 a.m.

✕ 通常用 nor 指出一種負面的 "state" 狀態, 如果後面的負面是
  名詞、形容詞. 或副詞片語, 就不用 nor, 改用 or

→ She is not interested in english or math.

→ She didn't speak slowly or clearly.

94

Questions 8: Write an opinion essay

*genocide 種族滅絕, 集體屠殺
→ The systematic and widespread extermination or attempted extermination of a national,
*antipathy 反感, 厭惡 to/toward 答題範例 racial, religious, or ethnic group.
for/against → He felt a strong antipathy towards them.

Question 8 *overlook ① 眺望, 俯瞰：The house on the hill overlooks the valley.
② 看漏, 忽略 ③ 細看, 檢查 ④ 寬恕：He has been kind enough to overlook my fault.

My question would be for Adolph Hitler, and it would appear to be a very simple question,

but it is actually quite complicated. The question would be why? What happened in your

life that led you to believe that a certain group of people, the Jews, deserved to be /dʒuː/ 猶太人

exterminate v. 根除；殲滅；消滅
exterminated? And what gave you the right to think that you should be the one to carry

carry out 執行；進行
out this genocide? I don't have any questions about how you carried out the Holocaust—

that's been explained by the history books. I want to know what happened to you 納粹對猶太
的大屠殺
放放句首, 例顛
personally that made you hate Jews and try to kill all of them? Not just the ones that did

you harm. All of them. 你徹底的瘋了 comprehend 理解
→ comprehensible adj. 理解的
utterly 完全地, 徹底地：You are utterly mad! no

I want to know because I find it utterly incomprehensible for one human being to have

人, 同胞
such violent antipathy toward his fellowman. After all, no matter who we are, we're all the

想像, 設想 更不用說, 遑論
same flesh and blood. I can't conceive of wanting to kill a single person, let alone an
民個的, 民族的 *ethic 道德原則
entire ethnic group. Surely, even if there were a few bad Jews, how could you overlook

① 計作, 種體 ② 普遍來說
their contributions to society as a whole. Jews have done many, many great things for

人類, 人道 無疑地 接管, 施任
humanity. Certainly, they weren't starting wars or trying to take over Germany. Thus, I

think something happened to you early in life. Maybe you were ashamed of the fact that

n. 遺產, 繼承物, 傳統 n. 血系
you had Jewish heritage in your family lineage. That's right. You were part Jewish. So,

something terrible happened to you, and I want to know what it was. I think everybody in

the world should know so we don't let it happen to some other kid who may grow up to

n. 人類 This meat is not fit
adj. 人的, 人類的 for human
wipe out a different group of people. consumption.

→ He treated the prisoners with humanity. 以人道對待罪犯人

Mostly, I would want to ask this question because it's a very human question. It goes

n. 衝突, 抵觸, 不一致, 分歧
right to the heart of your conflict. I'm awfully sorry you had to live the life you did, but I'm

adj. 缺乏知覺的, 毫無意義的, 無知的
even more sorry for the millions of lives you so senselessly destroyed. 這種肉不適合人類食用